The noise of the alarm cut through the peaceful darkness of sleep like wind heralding a winter storm. I reached over to smack the snooze button and hit the bedside table. I'd been up half the night so I had moved the alarm to my dresser to prevent snooze abuse. Once I lurched across the room to stop the grating sound, I was upright and might as well shower and get it over with.

I refused to look at myself in the bathroom mirror. During the first foggy minutes of morning I could pretend I was still the person I'd seen blurrily during the late, dark hours when I was alone and safe. I wanted to be myself for a little while longer.

being emily

by

rachel gold

Bella
BOOKS

2012

Bella Books, Inc.
P.O. Box 10543
Tallahassee, FL 32302

Printed in the United States of America on acid-free paper
First published 2012

Editor: Katherine V. Forrest
Final Cover Designer: Judith Fellows
Cover design: Kristin Smith
Photograph credit: Sergey Smolyaninov

ISBN 13: 978-1-59493-283-0

For Elise Heise
and her wild and precious life

Acknowledgments

Many people helped make this book possible and while I hope to thank all of them here, I'm sure I'll leave out some people who deserve thanks. In addition, I read a lot of material while researching the novel and I want to be clear that any mistakes in the text are mine and not the fault of those excellent books and websites.

If you want to know more about the research, resources and people who went into creating this novel, please visit www.beingemily.com.

I want to thank many members of the trans community who were generous with their time and stories. This includes Kate Bornstein (who taught me to value my own femininity), my former roommate Scott, Debbie Davis of the Gender Education Center, the members of GenderPeace, particularly around 2004–05, and, of course, Elise Heise to whom this book is dedicated.

I also want to thank my family members who gave me emotional, editorial and material support: my mother and father and my great-aunt Rhoda. I am blessed to have a family that's almost as excited about this book as I am.

Thank you to my amazing co-workers who create the best corporate job environment an author could have—and particularly those who read and commented on earlier drafts of this book: Wendy Nemitz, Dawn Wagenaar, Liz Kuntz, Christine Nelson, Kathy Zappa and Sara Bracewell.

I'm also grateful to the members of my very long-running *World of Warcraft* guild, who don't care what gender I play, and who put up with me missing raids to finish the edits—and to the many gamers who have created GLBT-friendly places in game.

A huge thank you to my amazing set of last-minute readers for the final round of edits and my repeat readers: Jeni Mullins, Nathalie Isis Crowley and my dear friend Alia, who holds the record for reading the most drafts.

About the Author

Currently an award-winning marketing strategist, Rachel Gold also spent a decade as a reporter in the LGBT community where she learned many of her most important lessons about being a woman from the transgender community. She has a Bachelor of Arts in English and Religious Studies from Macalester College, and a Master of Fine Arts in Writing from Hamline University. For more information visit www.rachelgold.com or www.beingemily. com.

CHAPTER ONE

The noise of the alarm cut through the peaceful darkness of sleep like wind heralding a winter storm. I reached over to smack the snooze button and hit the bedside table. I'd been up half the night so I had moved the alarm to my dresser to prevent snooze abuse. Once I lurched across the room to stop the grating sound, I was upright and might as well shower and get it over with.

I refused to look at myself in the bathroom mirror. During the first foggy minutes of morning I could pretend I was still the person I'd seen blurrily during the late, dark hours when I was alone and safe. I wanted to be myself for a little while longer.

Under the hot stream of water I kept my eyes closed. It felt like I was washing someone else's body. Even after sixteen years I still had moments where I couldn't understand how I got here or how such a mistake could be made. I knew what I was, and this tall, angular body was not that.

As I scrubbed, I flip-flopped on my decision to talk to my best friend and sort of girlfriend. "Sort of" because Claire was dating the version of me that didn't really exist. I would spend the whole day going back and forth with that in my head, I could already tell that much. I liked her enough that I felt bad about deceiving her, maybe more than anyone else, and I guess that's one reason why I decided to tell her first. I had tried to tell two other friends in earlier years, but that hadn't gone so well. One stopped talking to me and the other laughed so hard I confirmed to him I'd been kidding. Maybe I should have stopped trying to tell anyone, but the truth welled up in me so thickly I knew I couldn't hold it back much longer.

Like every other morning that winter, it was still dark outside when I woke up and the window was just turning light when I got out of the shower. I had to confront the dozens of outfits that I could wear but didn't want to. Worn down by years of dressing up as a boy, I'd pared my clothing options down to one of three basic outfits: jeans and T-shirt, jeans and sweater, jeans and button-down shirt (for days when I was supposed to look dressy).

That morning I stood in front of my closet wondering what you wear to tell your girlfriend that the boy she's dating is really a girl inside. Grandma Em had sent me a cashmere sweater two Christmases ago that I hoped would give me some measure of courage. It was so soft and I loved the feel of it, even if the olive color wasn't one I'd pick for myself; it made my skin look gray. I put it on, ran my fingers through my hair and went down to get some cereal.

Dad was on his way out the door and he leaned against the wall to pull on his massive, thickly-lined boots. "Lookin' good, Chris," he said. "Swim meet?"

"Last of the season," I told him. "Claire's coming."

His eyes were unreadable. He wasn't sure if he liked her or not, but I think he was glad I had a girlfriend this year. He nodded, waved and slipped out into the snow.

In our house, the kitchen is to the left of the front door when you're coming in, and to the right is the living room, which turns into a den at the back of the house. The kitchen opens into an eating nook, just big enough for a table of four. The house used to be a three-bedroom until dad and his buddies built the addition over the garage that's my bedroom so he and Mom could have one bedroom for paperwork and crafts. On my way to the kitchen table I grabbed milk and cereal and mumbled a "good morning" to Mom, who was busy assembling sandwiches.

At the table, I poured milk into a bowl and then dumped a few cups of Cheerios on top. I don't know why people pour milk over cereal, it makes it get soggy so much more quickly than if you put the milk on the bottom first. Mom finished making our lunches and set the two bags on the table just as my nine-year-old brother, Mikey, blew into the room. His hair was going all sorts of directions, which he seemed oblivious to as he grabbed a bowl, snatched the milk from in front of me, and poured it over his heap of cereal until the whole mass threatened to spill over the side.

Mom tried to fix his hair while he was eating and managed to get the worst bits to lie down. "I'll probably be working late today," she told us. "But your dad will be home."

"I'm going to Claire's after the meet," I said.

"Dad's not cooking…is he?" Mikey asked.

Mom smiled. "No, there's lasagna in the fridge. Chris, what time are you coming home?"

"Eightish," I said.

"You make sure you get your homework done, okay? I don't want you playing computer games all night or whatever it is that takes up all your time."

"Yeah."

"Is Claire's mother going to be there?" she asked.

Claire is the only child of a divorced mother, which worries my parents for reasons I could not begin to imagine. I think they assume that Claire and I spend every spare moment we're alone at her house having sex and smoking pot while selling illegal weapons to Middle Eastern terrorists via the Internet.

"Yeah," I told her, though it was a lie. Claire's mom usually got home around six or seven at night. "She gets home around five." When I said it, my stomach tightened. So much of my life was a lie, I hated to add to that pile of deception.

I looked pointedly at the clock on the microwave. "Gotta run." I grabbed the lunch bag and stuffed it in my backpack, kissed Mom's cheek, and made for the front entryway.

Winter in Minnesota is its own creature. Like a wild animal, you have to treat it with respect, which includes wearing a down coat and huge boots from November through March. I toed the line on those items because I refused to wear a hat if the temperature was above zero Fahrenheit. With a little bit of gel, my hair naturally curled into loose brown waves, which I loved. Thanks to the popularity of Orlando Bloom and all of the long hairstyles in the *Pirates of the Caribbean* movies, I'd persuaded Dad that it was okay for me to keep it a couple inches long and for it to touch my collar in the back. A hat inevitably crushed the cute little curls, and so the hat spent most of winter on the closet shelf.

I looped a scarf around my neck twice and tucked the ends down into my jacket. Then I threw my backpack over my right shoulder and pushed out into the wind.

February is bleak the whole month. The days are short and cold, the nights are long and frigid, the snow is feet deep and the wind has a razor's edge. I'd turned sixteen last spring and Dad insisted on getting me a car. His passion in life is restoring classic cars. He offered me a Mustang, which I managed to dodge by pointing out a '56 Chrysler 300B in bad shape that we could restore together. Granted I had to spend the summer working on a car with my dad while he called me "son" every five minutes, but on the bright side, I got to drive a tri-toned, candy apple red, chromed-out car that looked classy, rather than the dirt-ball Mustang I-watch-pro-wrestling-mobile.

The car definitely helped my reputation around school as a cool kid, and Claire reminded me weekly how lucky I was. I was a good-sized kid for my age, a little above average for the guys in my class and much too above average for the girls, while Claire described herself as "a runt." She's 5'4" and skinny. I tried to tell her that if she'd just stop dyeing her hair goth-black, she might have better social standing, but she just accused me of not understanding girls. Girls, she explained, are mean. If it wasn't her hair that stood out, the rest of the girls would find another reason to pick on her.

"I'm just an outcast," she said. "They're like wolves; they can smell it on me."

My car was an ice block when I started it, and I sat in the driveway for about five minutes, freezing my butt off while it warmed up. I could have gone back in the house, but Mom would try to have a conversation with me about school or Claire. She and Mikey would be out in a few minutes so she could drop him at the elementary school on her way to work; she's the secretary for a financial planning office. Most days she works from nine to three, but once or twice a week they keep her later.

When the car was warm enough, I pulled out of the driveway and pointed it toward school. Like a well-trained horse, it knew the way and drove itself while I listened to the radio. In Liberty we get four stations, two from the Cities and two Christian stations. That meant my choices were "Top 50" and "Hip Hop/Dance." I chose the latter.

Liberty-Mayer High School served parts of three counties west of the Twin Cities and had about five hundred students in a long, low, tan brick building. Being in Minnesota we had about twelve students of color and the classes were, for the most part, equally colorless. I pulled into the student lot and slogged across three hundred feet of trampled snow to get to the front doors. A blast of hot air hit and made me peel off the scarf as I headed for my locker.

A couple of the guys on the swim team shouted greetings and I yelled back with the automated voice program that takes over as soon as I get to school. I hardly have to think about it anymore. My larynx is programmed with all the appropriate responses, and I don't even pay attention. It's like I wrote all the code years ago and now my brain just reads it:

/run: greet teammate
1. speak: "Hey man, how's it going?"
2. joke about: a) sports, b) cars, c) weather, d) class
3. make inarticulate sound of agreement
4. run line 2 again
5. make gesture: a) grin, b) shrug, c) playful hit
6. repeat 3–5 until bell rings

My mornings are drab. I start with science, a scheduling glitch that is an offense against all night owls, and then go to American history. Between history and study hall, I usually pass Claire in the hall and she tucks a note into my pocket.

That day the note said: "Hey boo, are we on after the meet? Mom's working late. I'll see you after school." It was just a small piece of notebook paper, but my heart started racing again.

Sitting in the library for my study hall, I tried to concentrate on schoolwork, but I really wanted to figure out how the hell I was going to talk to Claire. I had plenty of "friends" from the guys on swim team to various kids I had class with, but Claire was the only person I felt excited to see on a regular basis. With the other kids it was just too hard to keep up the pretense of being Chris all the time. My life could be worse, and if I lost my relationship with Claire, it would be. I didn't know how much worse I could handle, but if I didn't talk to someone soon there wouldn't be any of me left at all.

Claire breezily described herself as bisexual and she was the weirdest person other than me that I knew, but at times I thought the bi thing was just her attempt to be unique. She'd never had a relationship with a girl…well, other than me, but I didn't really count because I looked like a boy to everyone.

I stared at the distant sky outside the gray library window. What was the worst that could happen? She could dump me and tell everyone at school and my parents. Then I'd either have to lie and say I made it all up as a joke, or run away. Or I could kill myself. I know that's a really morbid thought to have, but somehow it always comforted me. If it didn't work out, I could just opt out. Knowing there was a way out of even the worst situation made it possible for me to have a lot more courage. I didn't want to die, but I certainly didn't want to go around pretending all the time for the rest of my life either.

There was no way I could use the library computers to look up anything to help me come out. I'm sure the school monitored our computer use, and some other kid would probably walk by. All I needed was for one of the swim team guys to see COMING OUT AS TRANSSEXUAL in huge letters over my shoulder.

I opened my math book and made my eyes focus on the hardest problems I could find. That distracted me until the bell, and then math class itself kept me occupied until lunch. Unfortunately, Claire pulled fourth period lunch this year, so I usually sat with the swim guys or did homework at the table.

After lunch I felt pretty tired and I was trying to figure out if I could sleep through my sixth-period psych elective. The teacher was cool, but we'd been talking about schizophrenia for most of the week and I was over it. I leaned back in my chair and was preparing for an eyes-open doze when Mr. Cooper wrote two alarming words on the board: "Sex" and "Gender."

"Can anyone tell me the difference between these two?" he asked.

Mr. Cooper was a tall man with messy red-brown hair that my Dad would call much too long, even though it only covered his ears and the back of his neck. He had that super pale Irish coloring and a case of ruddy windburn on his cheeks, so I couldn't tell if this subject was making him blush as much as it made me. He stood with his hands clasped behind his back, which made his small gut stand out, and he shifted his weight from left to right and back again, but his eyes swept over the class calmly.

I could answer his question, but no way was I opening my mouth. A football kid in the front row volunteered, "Sex is what you do, gender is who you're doing it with."

Laughter all around.

Jessica, the blond girl who sat next to me and I think had a crush on me, rolled her eyes. "What a jerk," she whispered.

"For the next two weeks we're going to look at different aspects of sex and gender," Mr. Cooper said. "I'm going to hand out permission slips you need to fill out in case any of your parents don't want you to hear about sex, as if that will stop you. We will be talking about normal and abnormal sexuality, and we'll have someone coming from the Gay and Lesbian Action Center."

I thought about putting my head down on my desk and crying, but then that would probably give me away as being the wrong gender. I pushed the permission slip into the front of my psych book. I'd forge the signature in study hall tomorrow. That was one conversation I didn't want to encourage with my folks.

Mr. Cooper spent the rest of the hour explaining how sex often referred to a person's physiological characteristics, while gender pointed to the psychological, cultural and learned aspects. I could have taught the class. Instead I sat very still and felt like someone wrapped one hand around my heart and with the other hand crushed my throat.

CHAPTER TWO

English saved me. I had a chance to recover while Ms. Judson lectured on 19th Century British writers. Claire met me outside the classroom door when we were done and gave me a quick hug and a kiss on the cheek. I must have held her too close because she looked at me searchingly.

"You okay?"

"Long day," I evaded.

"I'll see you at the meet," Claire said. "I'm driving over with the yearbook staff so we can have our meeting on the way."

Despite her protests about being unpopular, Claire was on the yearbook committee, in the drama club and in a poetry workshop that I sometimes attended. She said she got in the habit in junior high when her mom wouldn't let her come home early and now she was hooked.

Liberty-Mayer High School didn't have an indoor pool, so we swam at the city pool after school most days until 5:30 or 6:00 p.m. It was a great way to avoid being stuck at home with my family. I could get home in time for dinner, eat, and then go up to my room for homework until it was time to sleep.

Tonight was the last of the boys' swim team's regular competitions, and our last chance to qualify for sectionals. I wasn't the only one on the team convinced that we didn't stand a chance. We competed against a lot of bigger high schools with their own pools and a larger student base to draw from. Plus our team wasn't particularly competitive, which was another reason I stayed on it. Our coach always emphasized beating our own personal times over beating another team, though that may have been a tactic to keep us from getting too depressed when we didn't stand a chance against most of the other teams.

I didn't mind being in the boys' locker room any more than I minded using the boys' restroom at school. Actually the locker room was better because it didn't have the same level of disgusting graffiti. I don't know why guys are so obsessed with their junk that they have to draw it all over the stalls. Plus, I lucked out in not being attracted to guys, so the only part that embarrassed me in the locker room was changing into my swim trunks. I just turned into my locker and did it quickly.

Our team trunks looked like black biker shorts with the school symbol on the front of the right thigh and our colors up the sides. I pulled them on fast and shoved my clothes into the locker. Then I turned and smacked my shin into the low bench between the rows of lockers.

"Shit!"

Blake turned around a few lockers up and shook his head. "Again, Hesse?"

I had a reputation for knocking into things or tripping over my own feet just about every practice session. I did it at home too. My shins, knees and feet always had two or three bruises on them.

"It's for luck," I told him. "Part of the ritual."

He laughed. Blake was a senior and the team captain. He took an immediate liking to me last year when I said I'd swim the 500 freestyle because it was the event no one else on the team ever wanted to swim. He had wild, curly dark hair that stood out from his head in all directions, naturally tan skin and the best muscles on the team. At least a dozen girls at school had crushes on him, according to Claire.

I put on my cap and my goggles so that they rested up on my forehead. Then I wrapped the big towel with our school emblem on it around my shoulders like a shawl and followed Blake out to the pool.

There were a lot of reasons to love swimming and the format of the meets was one. Unlike football or basketball where most of the team is on the field the whole time, we spent most of the time sitting by the pool stretching and bullshitting. There were twenty guys on the team but at most we had four competing at a time. Those of us out of the water only fell silent during the races, which usually took a minute or two. Each guy could swim two to four events. I only swam two: one leg of a relay and then the 500.

The 500-meter freestyle is the longest solo swim of the meet— more than double any other. It's ten laps in the pool and covers about a third of a mile. I actually liked it, but the guys never believed me when I said that. Of all the events, it was the one where pure muscle strength was less important than pacing, endurance, breath control and strategy. I really had to manage how fast I swam the first six laps so that I had the right energy available for the last four.

It was also the most boring event of the meet. Watching guys flash through the water racing against each other for up to two minutes is exciting—watching that same thing for about five minutes really loses its thrill.

Our relay came early in the meet, and then Blake and I sat on the side of the pool and stretched. The 500 was always one of the last events and that gave me time to recover before I swam again.

"How's it going?" he asked and jerked his chin toward where Claire sat in the bleachers.

She looked like an inkblot on a bright painting. Three colorfully dressed girls from the yearbook committee sat with her in the middle of a larger, spread out grouping of family members, friends and girlfriends of the team. Shrugging, I rubbed my big toe around one of the tiny octagonal tiles that covered the floor.

"Do you like it?" he asked.

I looked up at his face. Blake got around, we all knew that, but he wasn't one of those guys who bragged about it. At least not more than usual. I knew he'd had sex with at least two girls already this year, so he couldn't be asking how I liked sex with Claire, could he?

"What?" I asked.

"Being with the same girl that long," he said. "You've been together like half a year?"

"Just over," I said. We'd passed the seven-month mark two weeks ago, but I didn't want it to seem like I paid too much attention to that. He seemed to be waiting for me to say more. I had to split my mind into two halves—one half held all possible real answers to his question and the other half pretended to be him and scanned the answers to find the acceptable ones.

/error scan: boy test
    for each answer string (item in list)
    if item sounds like girl—discard
    else—echo item
        1. test "I feel at home with her"
        2. discard—sentimental
        3. test "I don't have to do as much work"
        4. echo
        5. test "I like the emotional intimacy"
        6. discard—major boy fail
        7. test "she's a sure thing"
        8. echo

"It's easy," I said. "I mean, I know what she likes so I don't have to work at it. And she's a sure thing." Guilt lurched through my gut. My relationship with Claire was so much more than that. With her I felt more myself than I did with anyone. Sometimes when we were flopped out on her bed together reading a poem and talking about it, I forgot that I had to play a boy and got to be a person for a while.

I couldn't tell her. I couldn't risk losing that.

"You don't get bored?" Blake asked. "Or look at the prettier girls?"

"Pretty girls are a lot of work," I said.

"Ha!"

They called the 500 and I got up, leaving my towel next to him. My head spun with thoughts of talking to Claire.

When I started on the team, Blake was swimming the 500 and he told me the trick to it: have two songs cued up in your head. The first song has a good steady pace and the second song is a little faster.

I didn't have a waterproof MP3 player, but I listened to my songs whenever I did strength training. When I hit the water, I started Beyonce's "Irreplaceable" in my mind.

The upbeat R&B rhythm of the song gave me a moderately fast pace.

The problem was I really wanted tell Claire. How bad could it be? No, that was a terrible question to ask because it could be awful if I misjudged and she told everyone and stopped speaking to me. What if I was replaceable to her? I couldn't tell her.

By the start of lap five I was trailing badly. Obsessing while swimming was a terrible strategy. I switched to my second song early. "Girlfriend" by Avril Lavigne.

Well that is what I wanted—to be Claire's girlfriend.

Hitting the second to last lap, my lungs burned and a dull fire ran along my arms and legs. In the water, feeling my whole body didn't bother me. The soft pressure reassured me of my reality. The water didn't judge. I pushed hard into the pain.

Fifteen seconds behind first place. Not bad. The coach slapped me on the back as I climbed out of the pool.

"Good swim, Hesse, you really picked it up. That's your best meet time."

"Thanks."

I stumbled back over to Blake where I sat against the bleachers and tried to catch my breath. My time wasn't good enough to go to sectionals. Even the guy in first wasn't going to do well against the stronger teams from the Cities. But the time was good for me and all the effort had cleared my mind.

I had to tell Claire.

***

"Go chill at my place, I'll be there in less than an hour," Claire told me when the meet was over. I was glad she didn't drive with me because I didn't know how I'd manage small talk when I had something so important to say.

Unbeknownst to any of our parents, Claire had given me a duplicate key for her house so I could go wait for her when her extracurricular activities went longer than my swim practice. Her house was on the other side of town from mine, all of a mile-and-a-half apart, but she thought it would be silly to have me go home for an hour and then meet her at her place, so she copied her key.

Her house was nothing like mine. First of all, it was tiny and in the well-to-do part of town that bordered on our one lake, and therefore more expensive than my family's larger house. Secondly, it was obsessively neat. At our house, Mikey or Dad always left junk around in the living room and kitchen, and Mom complained periodically and instituted weekend cleaning times, but it was never finished and tidy. Claire's house looked like a furniture showroom. Even the bookcases were designed more as works of art than functional pieces; each shelf held a few books and then some small statue or knickknack or a picture turned at an angle for effect.

Her mom worked at a flooring and countertop store and helped people pick out expensive tile and granite for their fancy houses. This house had simple wood floors, but the kitchen did boast the yummiest counters I'd ever seen, black stone flecked with reflective bits of other colors. Claire's mom made a good living and still got money from Claire's dad, who lived in St. Louis, so Claire rarely wanted for anything. She didn't have a car, true, but she did have her own TV in her bedroom and a Mac G5 desktop with a blazing-fast Internet connection and a monthly online game subscription to *World of Warcraft*. She let me have three of her character slots, so I logged on and fired up my level 85 Mage, Amalia.

Sometimes these online games got tedious for all the monsters a character had to kill to get to a new level, but it was more than made up for by the great gear I could buy and make, and the cool spells I could cast. Claire didn't have the patience to play magic-users, but they were my favorite. I admit, the fact that they always wore robes figured into that preference.

When I logged into the game and selected Amalia on the character screen, I could turn her 360 degrees and admire how awesome she looked. She always had beautiful long hair and sometimes I got it styled in one of the game's barbershops, but then it was flowing free all the way down her back. Her robes hung gracefully around her figure in violet and gray hues with gold tracery. I pushed the button to enter the game as her and got to step into a world fully female.

While I moved her around the city, I felt what it was like to be in her body. Some of the characters in the city were other players like me, but the computer created all the shopkeepers and city guards. They called me "m'lady" and simple as it was, that made me grin.

I was shopping for a new mage's robe when I heard the key in the door. "Hi honey, I'm home," Claire yelled from the entryway. I immediately started sweating while my skin went cold, which didn't seem fair. My body should have picked one or the other, but instead I ended up a damp popsicle.

I heard the thomp of her boots coming off. Claire had three pairs of thick, black boots that she rotated through in the winter. Each pair made her at least two inches taller, but when she appeared in her bedroom doorway she was her usual petite self. Today she wore a black crewneck sweater and black jeans with a bunch of silvery bracelets around her right wrist and a silver cross hanging down the front of her sweater. Her entire wardrobe was black. She once told me she started it when other girls teased her about trying to look fashionable in the eighth grade. Not only could she avoid those taunts ever again, but this look let her get away with wearing an ornate cross and no one knew if she was really serious or not.

She was serious about her own brand of radical Christianity. From time to time she could even come up with a surprisingly contextual Bible quote. The one she liked to give people who hassled her about her all-black, heavy eyeliner look was: "Do not let your adorning be external—the braiding of hair and the putting on of gold jewelry, or the clothing you wear—but let your adorning be the hidden person of the heart with the imperishable beauty of a gentle and quiet spirit, which in God's sight is very precious." That shut people up really fast and was pretty fun to watch.

I gestured toward the computer screen. "Amalia's got a new robe," I said, trying to sound normal while my tongue stuck to the roof of my mouth. "Plus120 Intel."

"Sweet, and it shows off her cleavage. She's hot," Claire said, trying to trip me out, like I'd care. Wow, was I about to test her true coolness factor. With a silent prayer, I logged out of the game.

She put her arms around my shoulders from behind and kissed the side of my face. "Mom's not coming home for a few hours," she said quietly, running one hand across my chest.

Our relationship had been getting more sexual over the last few months, and I had the distinct impression that Claire liked it a lot more than I did. To be fair, I'd like it a lot better if I had the right equipment. We hadn't gone "all the way," but at this point we'd done a lot of other things, some working better than others since I had trouble connecting with my body. She'd been sexual with a couple of other people and said I was the least selfish guy she'd ever met, which I suppose was a compliment.

Claire spun my desk chair around to face her and sat down on my lap. It would've been a lot easier to just let her talk me into fooling around, but I really had to have this conversation with her and if I waited, I was only going to feel worse.

"Can we talk about something?" I asked.

She ruffled my hair with her fingers. "Whatever pops up," she quipped.

I don't know what look I had on my face, but I suspect it was an echo of the crushing feeling I had in my chest because her eyes opened all the way and she stood up. "What's wrong?" she asked. "What happened?"

"Sit down," I said, which was stupid because her eyes got even wider.

She sat on the edge of the bed. "Are you sick?"

"No," I said quickly.

"There's someone else?" Those bright golden-green eyes narrowed.

"No."

"You're gay," she declared, leaning back on her hands and kicking my shin lightly. "I knew it. Of all the luck."

"No. Claire, let me talk."

She sighed and flopped all the way back on her elbows. Claire had this fantastic mass of black hair that spilled down her back. I loved to play with it. Unfortunately, what she didn't know was that half the time I was thinking about what it would be like to have hair like that. She complained about it frequently: how long it took to dry, how hard it was to keep it from frizzing out, what a pain it was to dye it goth-black when her natural color was a mousy brown, but she never made a move to cut it off. Lying back on the bed with her hair spread out behind her, she looked like a pixie with small bones and big eyes. I offered a quick prayer to anyone who was listening that she could understand what I was going to try to tell her. My brain kept coming up with things to say, but my mouth wouldn't cooperate because everything sounded so idiotic.

"You're sure you're not gay?" she asked while I struggled. "I mean, it's okay if you are, though I'll be a little upset 'cause I like fooling around with you."

"I like girls," I said through my constricted throat.

"And me in particular?" she asked. "Did you screw around on me?"

"No, again no, give me a minute." I couldn't really breathe, but now that I'd gone this far, I had to keep going.

"Chris, you're kind of creeping me out here," she said, but then stared up at the ceiling. "I'm shutting up."

Time stretched into an infinite plane. I thought about just running, standing up and going for the car, driving until I got to Minneapolis and never coming back. Then I considered telling her I was gay after all, but then I'd lose her and gain nothing. It wasn't too late, I told myself, just jump her, she'll eventually forget the whole thing. But she wouldn't. Claire was not only smart, but she remembered entire conversations weeks after they happened. You could not get anything by her.

Claire sat up straight again and opened her mouth. I didn't want to have to bat down another false guess.

"I'm a girl," I blurted. It wasn't the elegant explanation I'd intended, but I had to start somewhere. As soon as I said it, I blushed and couldn't look her in the eye, so I stared at the left side of her jaw.

Claire cocked her head to one side and blinked, her eyebrows drawing close to each other. Her mouth opened and closed and opened again.

"What?" she said with a sideways shake of her head.

The iron fist in my throat eased now that I'd started. "Ever since I was a kid I've known I was a girl," I said. "But I got stuck with this body. I thought God made a mistake, and I kept waiting for Him to fix it." I ran my hands down the front of my chest. "This isn't who I am."

Her face was white enough that I worried she was going to

faint or something, but she reached toward me with one hand and laid it alongside my cheek. Then she traced her thumb down the line of my nose and across my lips. She put her fingertips between my collarbones and ran them down to my sternum.

"How?" she asked.

I didn't know if she was asking how I knew or how I planned to fix it, but I wanted to answer that first question, so I did.

"When I was about seven, Grandma Em sent me a set of books for Christmas," I began.

I told her how the set included *The Wonderful Wizard of Oz*, *The Marvelous Land of Oz*, and especially *Ozma of Oz*. The first book was cool, Mom rented the movie and we watched it, but the second and third were a revelation. In them a young boy, Tip, escapes a wicked witch and goes off on an adventure to find the missing Princess Ozma. At the end of *The Marvelous Land of Oz* it's revealed that Tip is Ozma—that the princess had been bewitched into a boy's body and now would be restored to her rightful self.

I remembered how the first time I read that scene an electric shock traveled from the hair at the very top of my head down to the soles of my feet. In the scene, Glinda asked the witch, "What did you do with the girl?"

And the witch said, "I enchanted her…I transformed her— into—into a boy!"

At first Tip protests but Glinda says very gently, "But you were born a girl, and also a Princess; so you must resume your proper form, that you may become Queen of Emerald City."

I told Claire how I'd read the scene over and over again. How I searched everywhere in my life for the magic to turn me back into my rightful self. I knew I was born a girl, and I wanted so badly to resume my proper form as Ozma had. Claire closed her mouth and her eyes turned down at the corners.

"How old were you again?" she asked.

"Seven or eight," I said. "I knew even before that, though. I mean, I knew I was a girl. In kindergarten, I kept lining up with the girls when it was time to come in from recess and the teacher would make me go over and get in line with the boys. Before I was about five it didn't really matter if you were a boy or a girl, but as soon as we started getting divided up, I knew I should be with the girls."

"So what…what happened next?" she asked.

"I tried harder to be a boy," I said. "I thought maybe I'd just missed something, that maybe everyone has to work at it, so I had Dad teach me about cars, and I went out for the swim team, and I hung out with guys and did what they did. And after about six years of that I started to think that I'd become a very good fake."

"But you're one of the sweetest guys I know," she said. "I always thought you might be gay. You're so…" She trailed off.

"What?"

"…different from the other guys," she finished. "I mean, there's the cars and the swimming and stuff, and you look like a really cute guy, and your parts work—" She gestured at my crotch, causing me to reflexively cross my legs. "But you don't talk like a guy. At least not when we're alone."

"Talk like a guy?" I asked.

"I don't know how to describe it, but it's just different. The only time you really talk like a guy is when you're mad, otherwise it's a little like talking to my girlfriends." She pressed the heel of one hand to her temple. "I think my brain is scrambling."

She stood up from the bed and stepped back a few feet across the room and stared. I watched her eyes travel up and down my body a few times.

"It doesn't make any sense," she said, shaking her head. "I don't understand how you can be that way."

"There are some good websites that explain it," I said and wrote a few on the pad of paper by her computer.

"How are you going to be able to live like that?" she asked.

"What?"

"It's not like you can turn into a girl or anything."

Her voice sounded distant and she was still standing across the room, away from me. I couldn't tell how upset she was just by looking at her. Was she in shock or was she taking this relatively well? I couldn't afford to let myself hope yet and so my answer came out harsher than I intended. "I can get a sex change," I said, the words hanging in the air like icicles.

"You're kind of tall for a girl."

I stood up. "I should probably go." I wanted her to contradict me and tell me to stay. I needed to know she was going to be okay with this revelation.

"Yeah," she said. "I'll see you at school tomorrow."

My heart clenched, and I went into the living room and put on my boots and coat. She followed and watched me.

"Does this mean we're going to split up?" I asked before I could stop myself.

Claire's face was still paler than usual and at first she only stared, as if I hadn't been speaking in English. "What?" she asked.

"Are we going to split up?"

"Chris, don't ask me that. I don't know." She sounded angry, each word bitten short.

"Well tell me when you make up your mind," I said and stepped through the door into the freezing air.

By the time I'd started the car and driven halfway to my house I wanted to turn around and take that back, but I was afraid I'd find her still standing in the living room and staring after me in shock.

When I got home I had no appetite, so I told Mom I didn't feel well and I was going to bed early. Up in my room I set my alarm for four a.m. and then lay down and stared at the ceiling. The conversation with Claire played over again in my head until I finally fell asleep.

CHAPTER THREE

CLAIRE

After she did the dinner dishes, Claire wandered around the house twice before settling into her room. She lay down on her bed and stared at the blank ceiling. *Chris thinks he's a girl*, sounded in her brain like a gong that rang and echoed and rang again. *Chris thinks he's a girl.* She didn't know what to feel. When he'd told her, she felt angry, and then sad for herself. But as he talked about it, Chris looked so relieved that all her own feelings kept turning into guilt.

Most of the time he was so sad or angry or under a dark cloud, and this afternoon as he talked to her, his eyes lit up from deep within, and then he'd relaxed with her in a way she'd never seen in him before. She couldn't begrudge him those feelings, but the whole situation was so awfully bizarre.

Could she ever stop thinking of him as "him," she wondered? That made her brain ache and tilt sickeningly sideways, so she sat upright on her bed and put one hand on either side of her face to try to hold her mind still. There had to be answers. Chris had left the address of some websites on the pad next to her computer. It was risky because Mom would probably wonder what she was doing looking at those sites, but she already visited gay and lesbian teen sites, and Mom would never suspect Chris was… whatever Chris was. She could say it was for a school project or something.

Her mom knocked on her door, waited for Claire to say "Yeah?" and opened it. "Want to watch *CSI?*" she asked.

Claire made herself smile. "I've got a lot of homework."

Her mom nodded and went back into the living room and Claire figured she was feeling lonely again. Mom's last boyfriend had been a dud and they'd split up before the holidays.

Claire called up the websites and read until her eyes burned and all the little optical muscles around them felt sore. When she closed her eyelids, her eyeballs wanted to drop backward into her skull.

The science was hard to understand, and she'd seen a lot of information about genetics and gametes that she couldn't wrap her brain around. What stood out to her was the fact that female bodies were the default setting for human beings. In the absence of the right amount of testosterone, a fetus in the womb would develop female. Also genetics weren't the final story, at least not the way they'd been taught during those two weeks of sex ed in junior high school. She thought everyone with XX chromosomes automatically turned out with a female body, but because of the impact that hormones and other factors had on fetal development, they could actually turn out male or somewhere in between, and the same was true for XY. Some people were even born with XXY chromosomes or XYY and in very rare cases XXYY.

The cause of transsexualism and the broader category of "transgender" wasn't known. "Transsexual" meant people who felt they were the other sex from how their bodies were born and "transgender" was a broader category that included all sorts of gender varieties. The words made her think of the singer and drag queen RuPaul. She liked some of RuPaul's dance songs, but she couldn't picture Chris having that kind of big hair and wearing low-cut outfits with heels.

Being transsexual was rare, but not as rare as she first thought. A summary of ten studies over eight countries found that one in about 11,900 to 45,000 people were male-to-female like Chris said he was. But then other sources taking data from the U.S., U.K. and India found numbers closer to one in 1,000 to 3,000. That meant there were well over a million people like Chris in the world.

Some people online said that thinking you were transsexual was all psychological, but others pointed toward a physical cause. Two studies performed on the brains of transgender and non-transgender people who'd donated their bodies to science had really interesting results. There was an area of the brain about the size of a grain of rice called the BSTc. When they examined the brains of the transgender women—those born with male bodies who identified as women—they found the BSTc was the same size as women born with female bodies. Men who weren't transgender had bigger BSTcs.

The study size wasn't very big. After all, how many people donated their bodies to science in the first place? But if the studies pointed to a physical truth, then it was possible that Chris had been born with a girl's brain but his body developed male. All this time he'd been thinking of himself as female when everyone else naturally assumed he was a guy. How weird would that feel?

Claire put her fingers to her temples and rubbed her sore head.

After a little more looking she found an actual website with photos of men who'd become women. Some of them looked funny, their noses or jaws were too big, but a lot of them looked really good and a bunch of them actually looked prettier than most of the women teachers at their school. A few were models or actresses, and some were scientists and doctors and stuff.

But she didn't want Chris to be a woman. She liked him as Chris, maybe a Chris who wasn't sad as he was now, but still the guy she knew. It made her feel sick to think about any guy turning into a woman, let alone her boyfriend. There were men and there were women and you couldn't just go from one to the other.

It just seemed unnatural. But when she'd started to wonder if she was attracted to girls as well as boys, she heard plenty from people who found that unnatural when to her it only made sense to like whomever she liked and not bother about what kind of person they were. Was it any different with Chris?

Sure it was, the back of her mind said. *We're talking about changing his whole body. You just like to experiment, but he wants to turn into a woman. Guys don't just turn into girls, the world isn't set up that way.*

Claire couldn't even understand how it could be done medically and wasn't sure she wanted to. In the articles online, there were references to surgery and often multiple surgeries. How could it be right to change like that if it involved all that medical intervention? Didn't that point to the unnatural craziness of it all? Who needed to take a perfectly good working body and turn it into something else?

And even more importantly, why would God create a world in which women could be born as men and vice versa?

She turned off the computer and sat on her bed. "God?" she asked in a whisper. "What were you thinking? Why would you make people transsexual?"

She talked to God a lot and sometimes God answered— or maybe God always answered and sometimes she was too boneheaded to figure it out. She'd been raised Lutheran, like just about everyone in these parts, but her relationship with God came from her earliest memories of Sunday school when she remembered Jesus as the kindest, wisest man in the whole world. At times she could feel Him near her.

She went to church sometimes, but she didn't always feel God there. More often she attended an open Bible study held after the regular service. She didn't believe in a literal interpretation of the Bible, but she did believe it was a divinely inspired text and a way to engage in a relationship with God. Maybe it was because she loved words in all their forms that it was easiest for her to feel God's presence when she read the Bible or even in the words of poets and writers.

Pulling her worn Bible off the shelf by her bed, she let it open where it wanted. Her eyes fell to a verse toward the end of the Book of Job after Job loses his family and his health and all his money. He cries out to God for a reason for all the bad things that have happened to him.

"Where were you when I laid the foundation of the earth?" God asks Job. "Tell me, if you have understanding. Who determined its measurements—surely you know!"

What was that supposed to mean? She read it again and tried to remember what the Bible study leader said when they studied Job. In the end of the story, Job actually gets to speak to God—if she remembered right, it was the last time God spoke directly to a human being before the birth of Jesus. That was a really big deal. The whole Book of Job was about testing the depth of Job's faith, just as this situation with Chris tested her faith in God's design. Job got to hear God answer his questions and came out of the situation with renewed faith.

While Job suffered, his friends blamed all his misfortunes on him and were basically jerks to him. That was the other lesson Claire remembered learning about this book. Job was a story about compassion.

If she could sum up what God was telling her, it was that some hard things that happened to people were beyond her understanding. What God made for the joy of creation, that was God's work, and if that included men who turned into women and women who turned into men, who was she to argue? Was she there when God created the world? No. Did she help to determine its measurements? No.

Her work was to have faith and not be a blaming jerk like

Job's friends. No matter how upset she felt, Chris didn't deserve to have her take it out on him.

In the next verses, God asks Job if he knows what the foundation of the earth was laid upon, "or who laid its cornerstone when the morning stars sang together and all the sons of God shouted for joy?"

She loved that image of the world being created and the sons of God shouting for joy. The world was made for joy. Did that include transsexuals? She didn't understand how it could, but maybe she didn't have to. Plenty of people in the world were going to be awful to Chris if he kept going down this path, and she didn't need to be one of them.

But Chris also asked if this meant they were going to split up. Not being a jerk to him was one thing but being his girlfriend was a lot more than that and she just didn't know if she still could. If he started to change his body like that, how could she still be attracted to him?

CHAPTER FOUR

The small, quiet alarm beside my pillow chirped once and was silent, but that was enough to wake me. I wanted to run over to Claire's house and ask her again if she was going to split up with me, but it was four a.m.

Avoiding the creaky part in the middle of my bedroom floor, I got up and slid the bolt on my door to the locked position. I'd installed the sliding bolt last summer and Dad let me keep it. He realized that I could only lock it when I was inside the room and contented himself in knowing he and Mom could still search for drugs, or whatever they looked for, when I wasn't home. He probably thought I'd put it on so I could masturbate without Mom walking in on me. Dad thinks like that. I wasn't going to argue as long as I had some measure of safety for what I really wanted to do.

When I'd come in from school that afternoon, I carried my backpack in and up to my room, along with a nondescript black nylon gym bag. No one paid any attention to it, of course, which was the point. I'd thought all this through to the nth degree, and the bag was not only beneath notice but it bore a luggage tag on it which had Claire's name and address.

At least up until I'd come out to her the day before, Claire wouldn't mind me using her name on the bag in order to throw my parents off the track of a secret; she was pretty sneaky herself and had taught me a few tricks about hiding files on my computer. Luckily I had the kind of parents who hardly knew how to turn the thing on, unlike Claire's mom, who had probably installed two kinds of cyber-snoop software to protect her one precious daughter from sexual predators online. Claire came over and used my computer whenever she had something "of a delicate nature" that she needed to research, and paid me back in tips about how to keep my parents in the dark.

The duffel bag had her name on it because inside it was a pair of girls' jeans, a long skirt, two sweaters, a cute hat, underpants and two bras. None of them were anywhere near Claire's size, but if they looked in the bag, my parents would never consider any possibility beyond the obvious explanation that the outfits belonged to Claire. Plus they had no idea that she hated hats.

I unzipped the bag and then habitually paused to listen. Silence. More silence. Chirping bugs outside, neighbor dog barking, distant sound of a car and the rapid thud of my pounding heart.

I shucked my pajamas. The next few minutes were the best and worst of my whole day: the worst because I felt like such a freak, and the best because I slowly became visible. I went from being a charcoal outline of a person to being a flesh and blood human being, my skin filled from the inside out as I arrived into my body and my life.

I put on the underpants and the skirt. Because I was into competitive swimming, I had an excuse to shave my arms and legs—plus it got Dad off my back about doing something I could letter in—but mostly it was the smooth skin of the swimmers that caught my attention. If they'd told me before my sophomore year that they shaved for meets, I'd have been swimming my whole school career.

I put on the bra and hooked it, filling the cups with cotton balls, because they were easy to have around, and I found it impossible to actually stuff a bra with socks the way girls did in books. Then I pulled on the short-sleeved sweater with the scalloped neck that was my favorite and set the hat on my head, tilted back.

The inside of my closet door had a mirror that I could easily avoid in the mornings, but now I opened it and looked at myself in the darkness. Subtle light from the moon filtered in through my unshaded windows and mixed with the light of my computer monitor. I preferred that to the bright overhead light that would reveal too many of the rough details of my face. In this dreamy light I felt whole.

When you're a little kid, you don't really think about what you are; you just are. Some of my happiest times were when I was four and five. We lived in a different town then, across the street from a blond girl named Heather whose mom would bring her over to play with me in the basement all afternoon. Heather's mom often marveled that I was such a quiet kid, so thoughtful, and that I played so gently with her daughter. It seemed natural to me. We'd sit in the middle of the basement playroom that my dad had set up, and she'd show me her dolls and we'd dress them up in the other dolls' clothes and drive them around in the cars I'd gotten for my birthdays or build them houses out of the empty boxes Dad brought home for me to play in.

"Isn't he such a sweet boy," Heather's mom said one afternoon. "He's made a house for the dolls." I didn't know who she was talking about, but I started to feel that something bad had happened and I didn't know what it was.

I ran into the laundry room and hid until Heather and her mom had gone. From then on, I was on the lookout, trying to figure out what had happened to make Heather's mom talk about me like I was a boy.

When I went to first grade, the problem started to become clear to me. The teacher wanted the girls to line up on one side of the door and the boys to line up on the other side. I lined up with the girls and she told me to get in the other line.

"I'm not a boy!" I told her.

She knelt down and took me by the shoulders. "Are you afraid of the other boys?" she asked. "Did they do something to you?"

"No," I said. "I'm a girl."

She laughed, right in my face, her breath dark and earthy. "You're funny," she said. "You're playing a game with me, aren't you? You're pretending to be a girl today, but I know you're a boy. Do you know how I know?"

I shook my head.

"Because of your name, Christopher. That's a boy's name, so you get in line with the other boys."

I got into line with the boys. She had said one thing I understood: "pretending." Something had gone wrong with the world and I had to pretend to be a boy until I could figure out how to fix it. I knew how to pretend.

When Mom came to pick me up, I asked if I could have another name. At six, I thought that maybe if I changed my name I could be a girl.

"Why don't you like your name?" she asked.

"It's a boy's name," I said.

"Yes," she said, obviously not getting it. "It's a good name for a boy. Your grandfather was named Christopher."

"I want a girl's name," I said.

She stopped the car and looked at me. She looked at me for so long that another car started honking behind us. Then she let out a long breath.

"Sometimes," she said. "Sometimes Chris is also a girl's name. It can be short for Christine."

I beamed. I don't know what prompted my mom to say that, but it was one of the best things she'd ever said to me. The teacher was wrong, I did have a girl's name. I was going to be all right. Ever since then I've heard my name as "Chris, short for Christine."

Of course it turned out the name wasn't really the core issue, and Mom didn't stop Dad from giving me a good whipping when he found me in her dresses a couple of years later.

My body is the problem. It's hard to tell people that you're a girl when everything physical screams "guy." Even in the semi-darkness, my reflection in the mirror had these broad shoulders and no waist. I inherited my mom's thick lips, but my eyebrows look like Cro-Magnon man. They'd probably look better if I could pluck them, but I'm not too old to get a good whipping from Dad, so I leave them shaggy. I can still see his face, the grim set of his lips and how quiet his voice sounded when he told me when I was eight to take off the dress while he pulled his belt free from its loops. I think we both felt ashamed afterward, but for very different reasons. I never wanted to be the kind of kid my Dad would have to whip, so I retreated into my dreams and stayed away from girls' clothes until this year when I was sure I could wear them in secret.

I turned away from the mirror and went to my computer. It was an iMac that I got off eBay for a few hundred bucks a year and a half ago. Although slow, it still had some life in it, and anyway it only connected to the Internet at a blazing 56K. I wanted high-speed access, but Mom and Dad wouldn't pay for it, and I didn't want to spend that much of the money I made helping Dad with his cars just to get online.

There were a few good communities online, but my favorite was called GenderPeace. Even the name was cool and the administrator described it as a place for people "in the process of surviving transsexualism" which I liked, because I didn't want to be "a transsexual," and be a woman stuck in a man's body my whole life.

I'd found the website last fall and had been hanging around on it for about six months. A few hundred members participated from all over the world and they gave really good advice and talked about their lives. I spent a few months lurking and just reading the public posts until I decided to create a free account and become a member. I had to sign in each time rather than being logged in automatically, because I erased any evidence of my having been there when I logged off for the night, just in case Mom and Dad suddenly figured out computers. I assumed I could never be too paranoid.

My user name was "EmilyCH" for Emily Christine Hesse. I thought I'd keep Christine in honor of my Mom's cool moment and the choice they made to name me in the first place, and I got Emily partly from my Grandma Em and, I confess, a little from Emily Dickinson.

A couple of days ago, a new thread caught my eye and one posting in particular from a girl whose online name was "Bratalie." In her profile it turned out her name was Natalie and she had already transitioned and was going to high school as a girl in Minneapolis, an hour's drive from me. First I had a gut-wrenching pang of jealousy. To be able to go to school as a girl, how amazing! But then I just wanted to know all about it. I'd sent her a quick note saying I was in Liberty, Minnesota, still living in boy drab, and asking what it was like for her to go to school as herself.

When I logged in that night, I saw that I had private mail from her.

"Hi Emily," she wrote. "We're neighbors! Liberty is out in the boonies, though, how do you survive? You should come into the City! We could have lunch!" She included her cell phone number in the closing, along with a few more exclamation points.

Between my excitement about Natalie, and the growing dread in my stomach about seeing Claire at school, I couldn't go back to sleep, so I stayed up posting on the GP board for a while and then doing my homework.

Twenty minutes before my other, loud alarm was due to ring, I erased the evidence of my web surfing, undressed, put my clothes back in the decoy duffel bag and dropped it casually at the foot of the bed so it would look like I didn't care about it. Then I crawled under the covers and waited for the alarm to ring while I looked at the stars through the window. I could only see a couple points of light in the murky, dark gray sky.

"You look awful," Mom said when I appeared for breakfast in my jeans and sweater number two.

"Yeah," I agreed. I didn't want to attribute it to Claire or she'd think we'd had a fight and possibly ask why. "I might be getting a cold."

She touched my forehead. "You feel fine, but I want you to bundle up." Then she turned back to the sandwiches she was making. "Chris, I've been meaning to talk to you about seeing a doctor for your moods."

"What?"

"You're so unhappy all the time. I want you to go talk to someone professional and have them help you."

I tried to figure out if I was supposed to fight about this or not. It really depended on the doctor whether it would be worthwhile. I settled for indifference, which always worked when I didn't know what to do. "Sure, Mom," I said.

"Good, because you have an appointment today after school. I want you to meet me here at three forty-five and we'll go over together."

Okay, that was my cue to get mad, which wasn't hard since I already felt like crying. She'd messed with my schedule without asking, that was a clear violation. "What? You made an appointment without even asking? Mom, what the hell!"

She closed a paper bag with a sharp snap and glared. "Chris, watch your language, young man!"

That shut me up, but not for the reason she thought. I

hated being called "young man" even more than "son." I took a deep breath. "You didn't even ask me."

"I'm your mother," she said. "Sometimes I can do things just because they're good for you."

I shrugged. On five hours of sleep for many nights running, I didn't have the energy to keep fighting. "Fine."

"Don't be late."

I stood up and automatically kissed her cheek though at that point I was honestly pissed.

I was already halfway to school when I realized I'd forgotten my lunch and would have to eat a dry hockey puck, or whatever the cafeteria was serving.

A doctor? Some kind of psychiatrist, I was sure, when what I really needed was an endocrinologist to put me on the right hormones. I felt a miserable disconnect between my body, which wanted very badly to punch something, and my heart, which just wanted to cry. My eyes burned but didn't actually tear up, which was probably for the best if I didn't want to get my ass kicked by the football guys.

When I rounded the corner of the main hall, I saw Claire standing at my locker with her back to me. Momentum carried me toward her for a few more steps and then I stopped. If she dumped me now, I would fall apart.

She turned and saw me, then pushed through the two dozen students between us, while I stood frozen in place. She was wearing her favorite black sweater with a cobweb design stitched around the elbows and a long, black skirt over her boots.

"You look miserable," she said.

"I'm sorry about last night," I told her.

"Sorry for telling me?"

"For my stupid question about us being together."

"Is that why you're upset?" she asked.

All I saw in her face was confusion, and what I really wanted was certainty that she wasn't going to break up with me. I didn't have the guts to ask again if we were still together.

"That and Mom wants me to go to a shrink," I told her almost inaudibly.

She shrugged. "That could be good."

The bell rang, warning us that we only had a minute to flee to class.

"Hang in there," she said.

I tried to smile, but failed pretty badly. She hadn't said we were still together. Was she trying to let me down gently?

CHAPTER FIVE

I stumbled through the day on autopilot.
/run: please teacher
    1. raise hand
    2. give correct answer
    3. repeat once per class
/run: lunch with the guys
    1. pick one parent—complain
    2. mention sports
    3. mention car
    4. joke about girls
    5. nod

6. nod
7. nod
8. grunt
9. nod

While that was going on externally, I tried to figure out how Claire felt from our brief conversation that morning. She hadn't said one way or the other if we were still going out or how she was dealing with everything I'd said. Was she freaking out and hiding it, or was she genuinely supportive? Did she want to break up with me and just not know what to say?

In psych class we learned how embryos are differentiated in the womb, which was a good distraction though I had to keep my eyes half-closed in mock boredom and remember to groan when the guys did. In the first weeks of gestation, embryos are all basically anatomically female, and then when certain hormones start, the undifferentiated material of the fetus turns into the female or male configuration. It was actually more complicated than that, but Mr. Cooper didn't get into it, and I didn't blame him.

Even as the fetus developed, it wasn't necessarily as clear-cut as simple male and female. Mr. Cooper didn't talk about it, but a small percentage of babies were born with ambiguous genitals, neither fully male or female. In the past doctors picked which one they thought the baby should be, but recently some had started letting the kids grow up and say for themselves what gender they were, which made sense to me. I wished I'd had a chance to tell a doctor that I was a girl and have them just work that out for me.

By the end of class I really wanted to talk to someone who would understand how I felt. I hightailed it for the door the minute it ended. The school lobby was a mess of sound, but I went for the pay phone anyway. I had no cell phone for the same reason I had no high-speed Internet: cha-ching. I crammed a bunch of quarters in the phone.

On the third ring, someone answered.

"Natalie?" I asked.

"Who's this?" she asked and my heart fluttered because she had a girl's voice, a little throaty, but clearly feminine.

"I'm from GP," I said neutrally. "You sent me your number last night. I'm the one in Liberty." I was hyperaware of everything I said because there were about a hundred students who could overhear me if they wanted. Of course none of them were listening, but I couldn't be too careful.

"Emily?" she asked.

"Um, yeah, I'm at school. No cell phone."

"Oh, you can't talk, got it. Do you have a car? You want to meet this weekend?"

"Totally."

"Saturday afternoon? Do you know where Southdale is?"

I grinned. "I can figure it out."

"Great, meet me at two in the lobby of the theaters. What do you look like?"

"Orlando Bloom," I said. "Only taller and a lot less cute. And my hair's lighter. You?"

She was laughing. "I'm tall with red-brown hair. I'll wear a black skirt and black boots and carry a flower or something."

"Hey, can I bring my girlfriend if she wants to come?"

"The one you just came out to? Your post was awesome! Of course, that would be great. She sounds fantastic! See you on Saturday!" She talked with as many exclamation points as she used in her emails.

"Cool," I said and hung up. Then I looked at the clock hanging over the big double doors of the school and bolted for my car. I drove it cold, groaning and complaining all the way, and skidded up to my house at three forty-five on the nose.

Mom came out of the house as I pulled up; obviously she'd been waiting just inside. I slammed my car door and crossed the icy front lawn, hands jammed deep in my pockets. She was still in gray slacks from work with her eyes madeup and little earrings glinting in the amber sunlight.

"You're pushing it, kid," Mom said as she locked the front door behind her and gave me a shove toward her car.

"Sorry, school's crowded when it lets out, you know. I don't have a clear shot home."

"No lip," she said. "Get in."

We drove in silence a couple miles to a low office complex.

On the second floor was a uniformly beige waiting room where we waited. Mom filled out a bunch of forms and then a man came out of an office and shook her hand. He was almost handsome, with short black hair that grayed in that dignified way over his ears, and steel blue eyes. The two elements that messed up his good looks were his really thick brow ridge, like seriously caveman thick, and the way his smile looked like someone had just pushed the sides of his mouth up with their fingers and he was trying hard to hold the shape.

"I'm Doctor Dean Webber," he said. "Thanks for bringing Chris in to see me."

He shook Mom's hand and then mine. His hand was strong and dry, but really smooth and I slipped out of it mid-shake.

"Thank you for fitting us into the schedule," Mom said.

He nodded to her. "I'll have him back to you in an hour."

Dr. Webber showed me into his office, which was big enough for a long couch, a couple of comfy chairs, a few folding chairs and a clunky coffee table. I sat down on the couch.

"Hi, Chris," he said, as if we hadn't just met in the lobby. "Your mother tells me you're not very happy."

I shrugged. He hadn't done much to sway me one way or the other to liking him or disliking him, but I erred on the side of caution.

"If I'm going to help you, you have to tell me what's going on with you. It's not unusual for boys your age to struggle with anger and sometimes depression. Your mother is worried about you, and I'd like us to have productive visits here. What you say to me is confidential."

Right, I thought, my ass. I had the distinct impression that it was confidential as long as it fit within his expectations. There was no way I was going to tell him the truth and trust him not to talk to my parents.

"I don't know what to say," I told him.

"Why don't we start with a small test," he said.

He handed me a clipboard with the usual depression questions that were on tests like this all over the Internet. Did I have a loss of appetite? Was I having trouble sleeping? Did I think about suicide? I answered it, putting in some positives and fudging the other answers toward the middle.

He looked at it for a few minutes, nodding. "What about anger?" he asked. "Do you have a lot of anger?"

Yeah, I wanted to tell him, but it's because of all the fucking testosterone that my mutant gonads are shooting into my bloodstream. "I suppose," I said. "I don't yell and stuff, but I can get pretty mad."

"What makes you angry?" he asked.

"My brother's a pest. Some of my teachers are pretty stupid." Oh, and did I mention that I'm stuck in the wrong body 24/7 and people keep treating me like someone I'm not?

"What about your father?"

His question cut through my thinking. Why did he want to know about Dad?

"Dad's okay," I said, picking at the round border at the edge of the couch arm. "He's a regular dad, you know. He's not home a lot these days, now that he has the building job."

"Has he ever hit you?" he asked.

I was on to his line of questioning. He thought I was all depressed and pissed off because I was abused and sublimating my anger at my father. I debated whether it would work to use the word "sublimating" out loud to him, but then he'd probably say I was transferring my anger at my father on to him. I'd read plenty of psychology books while trying to figure out what was wrong with me.

"No, not really. He whipped me a few times when I was misbehaving, when I was a kid," I told him, all of which was actually true. It's important when hiding something big to tell as many small, distracting truths as possible.

Dr. Webber rubbed his chin, which would have looked very distinguished except that his face was too square and smooth to really pull it off without looking self-mocking. "And what were you doing to misbehave?"

Wearing a dress, I thought. "I was going through my parents' stuff," I said. "I was eight, and I was curious. I think he had his porn stash in there or something." I went on spinning a story that was as close to the truth as possible without actually revealing the important details.

I went into my mom's closet a lot as a kid. I loved the way her clothes felt. I'd rub her dresses against my cheeks and sometimes I'd fall asleep in there. My parents thought it was cute. I guess they thought I was comforted by her smell, or the close darkness of the closet, both of which were true, but what I loved most was dreaming of the day when I would grow up and get to wear clothes like that.

One afternoon when they were out and the babysitter was watching TV, I figured I'd try some of them on, in practice for that far-off day when they'd be mine. In my kid's logic I'd already given up on changing my name as a way to change sex, but I still figured that when we grew up, Mikey would get all of Dad's stuff and I'd get all of Mom's stuff and when I got to wear her clothes for real, I'd become the woman I was supposed to be.

Dad caught me in one of Mom's summer dresses and that was the end of that fantasy. I stayed out of the closet from then on, but not because of the beating. What really scared me was the way Dad stayed quiet the whole time. The few other times he'd spanked me in the past, he'd talked through the whole thing, telling me what I did wrong and how he was sorry to have to spank me but it was for my own good and so on. This time he didn't say a word, and I knew I'd done something so awful he couldn't talk about it.

I told Dr. Webber that I was making a real mess in their room and didn't mention dresses. He nodded and made understanding sounds. I kept an eye on the clock and kept talking.

I was trying to draw these stories out as long as possible and fill up the hour. I told him about another time Dad gave me a whipping for stealing some of his tools and burying them out back of the house. Actually the tools were mine. Dad gave me a toolbox for my tenth birthday and I was trying to get rid of it, but that story sounded close enough. Dr. Webber kept asking for more details about how I felt, what I remembered Dad saying, and I paused as long as I could before answering, pretending to scour my memory for details about each one. The minutes ticked by.

At the end of the hour, Dr. Webber shook my hand and said we'd see each other again next week.

I got into the car and looked out the window, trying not to feel like I'd been kicked in the gut. Saturday, I told myself, that would make it all worthwhile.

"Mom, can I take Claire to the city on Saturday for a movie?" I asked.

I planned to go whether or not Claire would come with me, but saying that I wanted to take Claire made the trip sound less suspicious. If Claire didn't want to come, she'd probably cover for me. Or if she wasn't talking to me, at least she wouldn't be around for my mom to ask how she liked the movie.

"At night?"

"No, a matinee. We'll be back by eight."

"All right," she said.

I let out the breath I'd been holding. One more day of school and then the blessed weekend would be here and Minneapolis and Natalie. I really wanted Claire to come with me.

CHAPTER SIX

CLAIRE

She paced across the living room and into her bedroom and back to the living room again. Then she tried to stop. Then she paced again. Chris had gone to the shrink today, and she wanted to know what he'd said and how it went. If there was some psychological way for him to fix Chris's problem, she hoped he'd listen to it. Chris could be stubborn when he made up his mind on something, which was actually pretty rare.

When the phone on the end table rang, she lunged for it. It was Chris's number on caller ID.

"How was Dr. No?" she asked, recasting the psychologist as the villain from the first James Bond movie.

Chris laughed, but it was a sharp sound. "As well as you'd expect."

"How's that?"

"Lousy. He's no good. There's no way he's going to help." His voice was a low monotone.

"Come on, you don't know until you try," she suggested, trying not to let her disappointment show in her voice. Life would be so much simpler if this was something Chris could solve in therapy.

"He just wanted me to talk about how angry I am and if Dad ever beat me. He thinks I'm an abused kid with a bunch of pent-up rage."

"You are kind of angry," Claire ventured. He didn't show it often, but there were times she could feel Chris's body vibrate with tightly held frustration.

"Yeah," he said. "But now you know why."

"True." She sighed.

She wondered if she could get her mom to send her to a therapist for a bit. Maybe she could find one who did know what to do about a teen who thought they were transsexual. Even just having someone confidentially to talk to felt like a good idea, but then she'd have to talk about her own life too and her feelings about her father leaving and all of that. She didn't want to go digging around in there until it was time to write her memoir.

"Hey." Chris's voice brightened. "Want to go to a movie in Minneapolis on Saturday?"

"Why not just go to one out here?" Claire loved going into the Cities for any reason, but she didn't want to show her excitement too soon. Since she was always the one pushing for a field trip, the fact that Chris brought it up meant that he had something planned, and she wanted to know what that was before she got her hopes up.

"We're meeting a friend. From my support group online," he said.

"A transsexual? Really?"

"Claire!"

"What?" She tried to sound innocent, though she was a little embarrassed by her own outburst. Still, she'd never met a real transsexual before and she was curious.

"That's kind of…reductive," Chris said. "We're more than a one-word label, you know, and I think Natalie would rather be called a girl."

"Oh, yeah, sorry." She paused and wondered if she should apologize more, or if that was enough. "Okay, movie on Saturday."

They hung up and she stood and looked at the phone as if it was going to ring again and answer all the questions still chasing each other around her brain.

Chris talked about everything so naturally: being a girl, meeting another transsexual girl in the Cities, but it felt so alien to Claire and vaguely disgusting. She tried to imagine Chris with long hair and breasts and in her mind it looked so wrong.

Mom was out in the living room watching TV, so Claire dropped onto the couch with her. She'd learned long ago that if she maintained a certain amount of Mom-time every week, she could get away with just about anything. Her mom acted younger than Chris's parents, even though she was a little bit older, and often Claire felt like she had more of a big sister than a parent. That bugged her in junior high when life was tougher and she wanted a parent she could ask for help, but now she appreciated how she had so much more freedom than other kids at her school.

"I'm going to the city with Chris on Saturday," she said.

"Are you having sex with him?" Mom asked.

"Whoa, where'd that come from? No," she protested.

"Honestly, Claire, I want you to tell me if you are."

For a moment she considered what would happen if she said "Mom, he thinks he's a girl" but Chris would kill her.

"No, Mom, we're not having sex. We fool around and stuff, but I don't want to get pregnant or anything, that would be a real mess. Besides, I might turn out to be a lesbian."

Mom rolled her eyes. "I swear, Claire, you make this stuff up just to torment me."

"I thought that was my job," Claire replied automatically, but she was thinking about how her mom had no idea what a person could be tormented with. She wanted to be supportive of Chris, but she couldn't shake the nagging concern that he wasn't right, that all this stuff about transsexualism was wrong.

"Oh, I've seen this one before," Mom said, and Claire looked up as she switched the channel from *Law & Order* to *Law & Order: SVU*. Pretty much either of them could turn on the TV at any time and there would be some *Law & Order* show on. Mom could go for months sitting on the couch every evening watching crime shows, and then suddenly she'd decide she was ready to date again and be out almost every night of the week socializing with the women from work and trying to meet a decent man. Claire's money was on that happening in April this year.

Although the crime shows always followed the same pattern, that felt more comforting than boring. The contents of the stories were sensational enough that Claire found she could always watch one, so she settled back on the couch, glad to have something to take her mind off Chris.

Twenty minutes into the episode, one of the suspects was revealed to be a pre-operative transsexual. A bolt of electricity jagged through Claire. She looked upward and asked God silently, *Are you hinting?* Seemingly random coincidences like this were usually the divine trying to get her attention. There would be some message for her either in this show or the one right after it.

Of course the story was overblown, with the character having accidentally killed a man to protect her secret and then being sent to men's prison where she was severely beaten. At the end of the episode, she was shown being wheeled into the emergency room, bloodied and covered in bruises.

What was God trying to tell her? That there were enough people in the world who wanted to beat up Chris that she didn't need to be one of them? Or that the path he'd chosen was a dangerous one and he shouldn't take it?

As the credits rolled, she picked up her glass of water and took a long drink, and when she looked up again the image on the screen made her jump so hard she spilled half the water in her lap. The face speaking into the camera had no nose and only part of a mouth and the eyes were surrounded by what looked like a mass of melted skin fused into place. Claire's breath froze in her throat.

"I'm sorry, honey," her mom said. "I didn't mean to scare you I just wanted to show you this while it was on. It's amazing. This man was terribly burned as a kid, and now he makes films to help families of burn victims."

Claire stared at the man's ruined face as he spoke. He had a deep voice that didn't fit his hairless features. He was talking about how hard it was for his siblings to deal with the aftereffects of the fire in their home that had scarred him, and how he wanted to help kids with these kinds of burns just feel like normal kids. The longer he talked, the more Claire could see the person he was, the kind soul, rather than the terrifying face.

This was an imperfect world, one in which children could be burned and hurt, or even born into a body that was wrong for them. In this man's case his own tragedy became his life's work. Hardship was a way in which people could really connect with each other and could show their greatness. Maybe Chris would turn out to be like this man, someone who taught others how to deal with hard situations with grace and compassion. Or maybe his journey would take him somewhere else, but as she wouldn't blame this man for his scars, she wasn't going to blame Chris just because she felt afraid about transsexualism.

And that was the basis of it. Her reaction to the burned man's face showed her this clearly. She had been startled, and while her startled reaction to Chris's news had been slower, it was similar. A piece of her solid world fell away when he said he was a woman. The belief that men were men and women were women was a foundational part of her world—until it was gone and she found herself teetering at the edge of the unknown.

Underneath her initial disgust, and all that questioning and discomfort lay simple fear. Well, she could handle fear.

She went into her bedroom and pulled out her journal. She spent so much time on the computer she knew her mom would look for a journal there, so she kept hers in physical form and hid it among her books.

She opened it to a clean page and wrote out her fears:

What if Chris goes through all of this and he's wrong but he can never go back again?

What if I can't be attracted to him through this and we split up?

What if the rest of the school finds out?

What if tonight was a warning and God doesn't accept transsexuals?

If I keep loving him, what am I?

CHAPTER SEVEN

Though I generally liked the man, I avoided Dad as often as I could, because the older I got, the more likely he was to clap me on the shoulder and start a sentence with "Son." Anything that started that way wasn't going to end well. Nevertheless, he caught up with me on Friday morning, clapped me on the shoulder of sweater number three and said, "Son, I've got something you're going to like."

"What, Dad?" I asked, feeling like a poorly cast character in *Leave it to Beaver.*

"It's a beauty," he said, which meant either a car or truck. "A

1976 Ford Bronco. The seller's driving it out from the Cities Saturday morning. I thought you'd work on it with me."

Okay, guilty confession, I do think cars are cool. I'm willing to give that up if it prevents my entry into the world of official girlhood, but for the time being it's saved my butt with my Dad more often than I can count.

"Sweet," I said, letting some actual emotion into my voice. "I'm taking Claire to the city at one, but I'm around all morning."

He beamed and smacked my shoulder a couple more times, then sauntered off to work. When my dad was working, he was generally a happy man. The few times in life he'd been out of work were miserable for all of us.

I grabbed a few slices of bread and hightailed it out the door before Mom could appear and grill me about Dr. No again. I cruised through the school day, buoyed up by the thought of Saturday afternoon. Claire and I missed each other in the halls, but this was the time of year she started to get busy with all the clubs so I didn't worry about it.

I ran aground abruptly in psych class. Mr. Cooper handed out our assignments. The guys booed, and I forgot to join in because my mouth was hanging open while my heart threatened to leap up my throat in a mixture of excitement and panic. The assignment said, "Pretend you wake up tomorrow morning the opposite sex. Write a four hundred word essay about your experiences."

"Gross," the guy in front of me said.

"Neanderthal," Jessica said back to him. She turned to me and batted her eyelashes. "You wouldn't be a jerk about being a girl, would you?"

/run: emergency avoidance procedure
      System Failure

I stared at her blankly. "Uh," I said.

"If I were a guy, I'd show some of the guys around here how to dress," she said, clinching the fact that she'd make a terrible guy.

"Yeah," I said. "Funny." There was no emotion in my voice

and I could hear that it was missing, but I couldn't do a thing about it.

"It's not bad being a girl," she said, putting her hand on my forearm. She was flirting, of all things.

"Sure," I said and stood up as the bell rang.

"Jeez," she said. "You guys are all alike. You're afraid of anything the least bit feminine."

"Sure," I said again and bolted. The walls were a blur closing in around my head.

An assignment to pretend we were the opposite sex, who comes up with something like that? And how was I supposed to do it? My body was fading rapidly from a solid to an invisible membrane so thin that if anything brushed against me I'd split open. I would have to write about waking up as a girl for the assignment even though every morning, just for those few minutes between waking and having to move, I was a girl with no stupid physiology to contradict me.

I had to get out of the school building without looking like I had to get out. By force of will I kept my feet steady, past my locker, past the lobby, into the biting cold, my car, the key in the ignition. Wait for it to warm up. Forget English class.

Up until I was about nine or ten years old, I still held out hope that I would grow up to be a woman, even though the evidence was mounting against that idea. When the other girls started to speculate about what it would be like to get their period, I imagined that a period was the end of childhood, like the end of a sentence, and after that I'd get the right body parts. I was old enough to have given up on a magical solution, but somehow I convinced myself that my problem would be sorted out through puberty, that I would start to grow breasts and that thing between my legs would recede and I would become like the other girls.

It didn't help that my best friend at the time, Jessie, started to grow her breasts just before her tenth birthday. For years we'd both been flat-chested and then a few weeks before her birthday she snuck me into her room to show me the tiny bumps her breasts had become. We'd been comparing bodies on and off for a couple years, ever since she'd talked me into peeing in the woods with her on a park outing with our families.

"I want my breasts to start growing too," I told her. She looked at me like I wasn't a real person. I slammed out of her bedroom and didn't talk to her for a couple of weeks.

I thought about that incident over a year later when I woke up to find that my nipples ached and felt swollen. For days I floated on clouds. I was going to show her and everyone. But the happy feeling just dissipated. I didn't grow breasts. Instead I grew a couple inches in the space of a summer, my shoulders widened, and I started sprouting hair on my chest.

I drove over to Claire's. I couldn't go home. I didn't have swim practice and soon Dad and Mikey would be home. I couldn't let myself cry with them in the house. And I needed to know where I stood with Claire.

When I got out of the car I realized I'd left my coat at school. Fumbling the key into her front door, I pushed into the house shaking with cold. I planned to have a little cry and then wash my face and wait for her to come home so we could talk, but that planning part of my brain wasn't running the show.

I walked through the living room and into her room feeling like someone was crushing my chest, like I'd gone underwater and couldn't get to the surface. My eyes swung from side to side looking for anything that would stop this feeling. Without thinking about it, I opened her closet door and curled myself into the bottom. Ever since I was a kid hiding in my mom's closet, I've found comfort in dark, enclosed places. The small part of my mind that was still thinking told me I was being an idiot, a baby, a wuss, a fool and a dozen other sneers.

I leaned against the back wall of the little space and finally managed to cry a few of the thousand tears I'd been saving up from the past months. Wiping my face, I looked at my hands. My freakishly huge hands. I hated them. I hated this stupid body. Whose bright idea was it to make me a boy? Was it so hard to put a girl together? Did they just run out of girl bodies that day? Did

I do something miserable in a past life? Maybe I'd been Hitler or Stalin.

"Chris?" Claire called from the living room, and then a little closer. "Chrissy?"

God bless her.

I cracked the door and crawled out to see her looking down at me with wide eyes.

"Sorry," I managed, hating my deep voice.

She knelt down on the carpet and grabbed my hands. "What happened?"

"Weird stuff," I said. I cleared my throat and wiped a hand across my face again, managing to smear snot across the back of it. "Tissue?"

She grabbed a box off her desk and handed it to me. "You look terrible."

"Cooper gave us this crazy assignment, to pretend we wake up tomorrow the opposite sex."

She laughed. "Oh, that's rich."

"And then this girl in my class was…she was just joking about it, but I couldn't deal because I just—" My voice broke and tears started again. "I just want to be a girl so bad. Am I completely messed up?"

Claire put an arm around my shoulders and dragged me to her chest. After all the times she'd curled into me, it felt so weird to lean my monstrously huge body against her, but it was also wonderful to feel held.

"You're okay," she said. "You just have a girl brain in a boy's body. Which I think makes me a lesbian trapped in a straight girl's body."

I laughed and she laughed, and then I cried some more. When I finally sat up and blew my nose, I felt a lot more peaceful. That was when I saw that Claire looked worse than me. Her eyes were bloodshot and creased with tiredness.

"You look like you were up all night," I said.

"Pretty much. I think I fell asleep for an hour in the middle."

"Of what?"

She pushed up from the floor and I stood with her. Her bed was made, like usual, but with big wrinkles in the middle of the comforter and four books open on it.

"Binge reading," she said and grinned. "Come on, make me a sandwich."

We went into the kitchen together. Claire was a much better cook than me, but I had one specialty dish: the grilled cheese sandwich. I think it only tasted better when I made it because she didn't have to do any work, but she insisted I had a special knack.

"When's your mom coming home?" I asked.

"Late," Claire said. "She has a date and he's picking her up from work."

I wrapped the kitchen apron around my waist and tied it. Claire sat on one of two stools set up by the edge of the counter so people could talk to the cook. I put a big pan on to warm and pulled the bread, cheese and butter out of the fridge. The butter was the key ingredient. I believe that like popcorn, grilled cheese is just a fancy butter-delivery system.

"I've been freaking out," Claire said. "And I might freak out more, okay? But I think I'm good for now."

I took a long breath in. She wouldn't have asked me to make sandwiches or called me "Chrissy" if she was going to just throw me out, right?

"What does that mean?" I asked.

"Did you know that the Bible actually talks about transsexuals?" she replied.

The breath I'd taken didn't seem to want to come out now. "Um," I managed.

If she was going to get all right-wing Christian on me, I'd leave mid-sandwich. Claire had this kind of weird system of religious belief that I didn't really understand. My parents took me and Mikey to church every now and then, but we didn't make a fuss about it. Claire's family had taken her to church a lot when she was young and apparently she really dug it, but then when she hit her teenage years, she started reading *The Gnostic Gospels* and getting really into the early Christians and the formation of the Bible and all that. Then she read the mystics, which included St. John of the Cross and his cloud of unknowing, which she was always going on about.

I had no idea what the mystics thought about transsexualism.

"There's this bit in Isaiah," she said and hopped off the stool.

I turned the pan down because I wasn't going to start cooking the sandwiches yet, just in case I had to run for it.

Claire came out with her Bible and read: "For thus says the Lord: 'To the eunuchs who keep my Sabbaths, who choose the things that please me and hold fast my covenant, I will give in my house and within my walls a monument and a name better than sons and daughters; I will give them an everlasting name that shall not be cut off.'"

"Are you calling me a eunuch? Really?" I put down the spatula and started to untie the apron.

"No!" she said. "Just listen to me for a minute because this is really cool."

I stopped untying the apron string and folded my arms. The frying pan was probably getting too hot even at the lower burner setting, but I didn't care.

"Back when the Bible was written, the Romans didn't have a word for transsexual. But their word 'eunuch' included three categories of people. Only one of those is what we mean by 'eunuch' today. And one of the other categories includes men who chose not to procreate with women and those who dressed and acted like women. It includes transsexuals."

"You stayed up all night reading about this?"

She put the Bible on the edge of the counter and sat back on the stool.

"I was really afraid," she said. "I'm still afraid, kind of. I read bunches of stuff, about the brain studies and how there's actually a lot of transsexual people. Well, not a ton, but more than I thought. But, you know, nothing's more important to me than having a loving relationship with God, and I know people twist the Bible to say all kinds of crazy stuff. It's not like I'm a literalist, but I think that the Bible is a valid way for God to communicate with us. So when I read that about the translation of 'eunuch' and that passage in Isaiah, and there are others too, that's just the best one…I really got it."

I put the sandwiches into the pan and listened to them sizzle. "Good," I told her.

"It's not like I was looking for God's permission, like He's some kind of angry parent," she said. "The words just cut through my confusion and showed me what was already in my heart."

I had to ask. "Is dating me in your heart?"

"Yes," she said.

I grinned into the pan and flipped the sandwiches. "And you're never going to call me a eunuch again?" I asked, even though I thought her point about the quote and the translation was awesome.

She threw a dishtowel at me. It bounced off my shoulder and I tried to catch it on my thigh as it fell, but instead I ended up smacking my knee into the oven handle. I hopped on one foot for a second, holding the knee up, but it didn't hurt that badly and the sandwiches were about to burn.

I quickly slid the sandwiches out of pan and onto plates, then bent down to get the towel. Claire hopped off the stool again and took the towel out of my hand. She reached up and put her palms on either side of my face so she could pull me down to kiss her.

When the kiss was over, she smiled up at me and said, "Besides, I've always wanted to give lesbianism a real go."

I rolled my eyes at her and picked up the sandwich plates. "Couch?"

"There's a *Law & Order: Criminal Intent* on the DVR. Let's do it."

CHAPTER EIGHT

I slept for about eleven hours, which I'm certain shored up Mom's hypothesis that I was depressed, but to me it felt great. Then I spent about a year in the shower letting the water run over me. I shaved my arms and legs again, even though the swim season was over. If anyone asked I'd just tell them that the new hair itched and it was easier to keep it shaved. I would not mention that I loved the feel of smooth legs under my jeans.

Mom was cleaning up the kitchen when I made it downstairs, and Mikey was in the living room watching TV. He wasn't old enough to skip cartoons yet. I hoped that lasted another year because I enjoyed my Saturday mornings without him flying around the house like a pinball.

"How do you feel?" she asked.

"Great," I said. I poured a glass of milk and grabbed two of the cinnamon rolls she'd made. Mom seemed trapped between being a career woman and being a stay-at-home mom. I thought either one would be great, but she just wavered back and forth between the two, telling us to make our own dinner one night and then taking over the cooking for the next three or four days. "I've been up too late studying," I added around a bite of cinnamon, sugar and dough.

"Is school hard?" she asked, fishing for problems.

"Nah, I just want to do good for college aps." Which was true. I had no intention of going to college near Liberty and I knew Mom and Dad couldn't afford to send me anywhere fancy.

"Chris!" Dad yelled from the garage door. "Chris, come look at this!"

I flashed Mom a grin and grabbed my old jacket from the closet, wishing I hadn't left the good one at school.

Some fool had driven a junker of an old Bronco the fifty-odd miles from the Cities, his girlfriend following in her dilapidated Chevy. The Bronco was in terrible shape and looked about ready to drop parts into the street.

Dad and the scruffy man who'd driven it in were walking around it, looking under the hood, and then exchanging information and money. I was supposed to be in that circle with them, admiring the car and haggling over its value, but I just didn't feel like it. I could smell the guy from where I was standing and his lanky brown hair hadn't been washed in about a week. He smelled like burnt rubber and acidic sweat.

In the rusty Chevy, his girlfriend was smoking a cigarette, blowing long streams of light gray smoke through a one-inch opening at the top of her window and leaving enough smoke inside the car to make it hazy. I couldn't see her clearly, just the dishwater blond hair pulled back in a ponytail. What did she like about her boyfriend? Did she like the way he smelled and those skinny legs inside his faded jeans?

Dad motioned me over. "This is my son Chris," he said. "He's going to work on it with me."

"Chris," the man said. "You'll make your dad proud."

"Sure," I said, beginning to feel like that was the only useful word in my vocabulary.

Then he was gone in the smoky car with his girlfriend and Dad drove the Bronco into our oversized garage. We may not have had the biggest house on the block, but we definitely had the biggest garage, which was ironic since I always had to park at the curb to make room for the cars Dad fixed up. The garage was two spaces wide and a little over two deep and had enough heaters to keep it at least in the fifties during the worst of winter. Dad had installed four spotlights and there were times when the garage seemed brighter and warmer than the house.

Despite the fact that I was one hundred percent clean, I capitulated and helped Dad with the car. I had the feeling I was going to need a good stash of parental brownie points in the near future, so I pushed up my sleeves and got to work.

At noon I cut out, had a quick lunch, showered again, put on my second favorite sweater and went to pick up Claire. She slipped into the warm car and gave me a kiss on the cheek.

"Claire, what do you like about having a boyfriend?" I asked.

"I don't know," she said. "I mean, I'm not dating you because you're a guy. I like you because you're funny and smart and a total geek. And sure, I like that you're tall and strong and all that."

"But what is it about guys that girls like?"

"I think strength, for sure, and guys tend to be easier than girls, you know, less complicated...well, except for you. Guys make girls feel safe," she said and pushed on my shoulder with the palm of her hand. "I wonder if I'm going to miss that," she added quietly.

"I'll always be tall," I offered.

"Who's this Natalie?" she asked.

"She's from a forum online, a support site. She knows me by my girl name 'Emily.' Is that going to be weird?"

"Girl name?"

"I'll change my name legally when I can," I said. It was hard to remember that Claire didn't know that much about transsexualism, despite her long nights of study on the subject. She could sound so cool with it one moment and then completely clueless the next.

"To Emily?" she asked.

"Emily Christine Hesse."

"Is that why your mage in game is Amalia?"

"Someone already took the name Emily, and anyway, I like the game to be a little different from reality. But yes, I wanted a name that was like Emily."

She turned a little sideways in her seat so she could look at me more fully. "I played a male character for a few months," she said. "Like a year ago when I was really into player versus player combat. It felt like people listened to me more in the game when I was a seven-foot-tall guy. I thought you just played girl characters so you could look at their butts."

I laughed. That was what other guys in our guild said who played female characters. I was often surprised at how many of the female characters in the game turned out to be played by men in real life. I had no idea how many were transsexual or gay or really did prefer looking at a female on the screen while they played.

"I love that there's at least one world where I can just show up and be female," I told Claire. "It feels like magic to me."

"Like the *Wizard of Oz*," she said.

"Yes!" I agreed.

We both fell quiet for a few minutes and then Claire asked, "Am I supposed to call you Emily?"

"If no one's around, I'd like that."

"Huh," she said and went silent again.

We drove past snowy fields and trees decked in white and more and more houses until we came into the western suburbs of the Cities. Southdale was in Edina, which was a suburb and not Minneapolis proper, but close enough that my parents didn't make a distinction. Anytime I wanted to go to the Cities, they figured I was trying to score drugs or drink or something. Of course, Dad did a lot of drinking when he was a kid, so he didn't exactly disapprove.

This was one of those funny times when it worked out that people saw me as a guy. Mom and Dad didn't worry about me like Claire's mom did about her that I was going to get kidnapped or raped or sold into slavery. It must have been the crime shows they watched, because Claire's mom could fret for days about something catastrophic happening to her daughter but she never seemed to worry about where Claire actually was on any given day.

I pulled into Southdale and ended up driving around the mall twice before figuring out how to get into the parking lot in front of the theater.

"Man, don't you wish we lived closer," Claire said. She paused and grinned, "And by 'man,' I mean 'person' of course."

I smacked her shoulder. "Goof. Come on."

There were about two hundred people in the theater lobby. I was scanning, saying to myself "black skirt, boots, flower" when Claire grabbed my hand and dragged me over toward a girl. I thought Claire was going to ask for directions, until I realized the girl was wearing a black skirt and boots.

I couldn't stop beaming. She grinned back at me.

"Natalie," she said holding out her hand.

I took it, wondering at how soft it felt. "Emily," I said for the first time out loud. "But you should probably call me Chris. This is Claire."

"Hey," Claire said.

I looked Natalie up and down. She looked like a girl. She was a girl. She looked great. She wasn't quite as tall as my six feet, but she was a lot taller than Claire. Of course everyone was taller than Claire, even in her boots. Natalie had shoulder-length dark brown hair with red highlights and big, dark eyes that she emphasized with makeup.

"Come on," she said, taking my right hand and Claire's left. She pulled us away from the theater and down the mall to California Pizza Kitchen.

I tried to stop staring, but I couldn't stop watching Natalie out of the corner of my eye. She walked gracefully and if her hips were narrow and her shoulders broad and solid, they weren't more so than some of the members of the girls' swim team at my school. Natalie was so lucky to already be on hormones at seventeen, she could expect her body to pad her hips over the next few years. Her pelvic bones would always be narrow, but now her body knew that fat was supposed to go to the hips. We were probably the only two girls in the whole mall who wanted fatter hips.

At the restaurant, I took a chair across from her and Claire sat next to me. We ordered pizza to share, and the waiter called Natalie "miss" without a second thought. In addition to the long, styled hair and the pretty makeup, Natalie wore a tight-fitting tan sweater that made her breasts obvious. She looked like a solid B-cup to me, and I wanted to ask her if that was all from hormones or if she was augmenting with a padded bra.

If I looked hard, I could see how Natalie's chin was thicker than most girls, but the dark copper and brown hair falling around her face masked the effect and drew my eye away. She already had great lips, not the thin lips I'd been stuck with, and her makeup on them was a very subtle pale pink. Her cheeks fell in the mid-range; I felt a little surge of guilty optimism because my cheeks weren't as wide as hers and hers didn't read male because her eyes dominated that part of her face.

I had obsessed night after night over the pictures I could find online of women who transitioned. I scoured them for signs of maleness and tried to prove to myself that it was possible that I could someday live a normal life as a woman. But two-dimensional photos and even videos were nothing like the experience of sitting across from a real girl who'd been born into a male body. I wanted to touch her to make sure she was solid and not just a dream.

I had so many questions that I couldn't figure out where to start, so Claire took over.

"Look, tell me if I'm being rude at any point here, okay? We're the country mice, you know, and I think we have a lot of questions," she said. I nodded and Claire went on. "Can we ask 'em?"

"Sure," Natalie said.

Even that one word had a slight breathiness and lilt to it, putting it firmly on the feminine side of the line. Her voice wasn't high-pitched, but my English teacher's voice was a smokier, deeper woman's voice than Natalie's.

"Start with 'I was born a boy' and tell the whole story," Claire said.

Natalie laughed. "Well, it was the usual. You'll start hearing this a lot if you hang around us types."

"Wait," Claire said. "What do you call yourself? Is 'transsexual' gauche?"

"It's not great, at least in the sense that it kind of objectifies us and narrows us to that one thing. My whole life isn't about my gender identity, you know. I prefer to just be called a girl."

"But then how do you talk about it?" Claire asked.

"Some people call themselves 'survivors of transsexualism' or 'survivors' and some just abbreviate it and say T-girls, or TS, and some say transsexual, trans or transwoman. It depends on where you come from. I like 'girl' or 'T-girl' if necessary."

"That's cool, okay, go on with the story."

"When I was young I played with other girls, and I got upset when my sister got dresses for her birthday and I didn't. I played with her dolls, and by the time I was about six I wouldn't play with boys. Mom and Dad took me to two psychologists and one of them was really smart and said not to push me about my gender, just to make sure I had lots of all kinds of toys and watch how I developed. I told Mom I was a girl a few different times. She tried to explain that I was a boy, but I just wouldn't believe her.

When puberty hit, I started getting more and more upset. I mean really confused and sad and depressed. Some days I wouldn't get out of bed at all unless my mom made me. We went back to the psychologist, and Mom explained that I could choose to have a girl's body if that's what I really, really wanted. They put me on hormones a couple years ago and then we moved here a year and a half ago so I could go to school as a girl. It's been going really well and so this summer I get my last surgery and then we're all done."

"What surgery?" Claire asked.

Natalie raised an eyebrow and pointed under the table toward her lap.

Claire stood up. "Okay, I'm going to the bathroom," she said. "I don't want to know this part. Back in a bit."

Natalie looked at me. "She'll be okay," she said, though I think she was trying to reassure both of us.

"Yeah," I said. "So, wow, that's really cool about your parents. What's it like taking the hormones?"

"It's great. I don't feel so angry all the time, and it's easier to cry when I'm upset, and all my hair got finer and softer and my skin."

I reached across the table and touched the back of her hand. "It didn't used to be like that?" I asked.

"No, not that soft. It was like yours." She ran her fingertips down my forearm. "You shave your arms?"

"Swimmer," I said. "It's a good excuse to shave just about everything."

She laughed. "That's smart."

"Are you scared about the surgery?" I asked.

"A little," she admitted. "I just want it to go really well."

Claire came out of the bathroom and regarded us warily. I waved her back to the table. "We're done talking about that part," I said.

She looked a little sad but forced a smile. "So, do you like boys or girls or both?" she asked Natalie.

"Boys," she said. "But there are all kinds of sexual orientations in the T-community. I think sometimes it's harder for us who like boys to figure it out, because we can think we're just gay. But then if you like girls it's hard because you're going to end up a lesbian and some therapists don't like to recommend a sex change that's going to make another lesbian. They think if you like girls you should just try to be a boy."

The pizza had long since arrived and been more or less nibbled to death. I took another piece and put it on my plate, though I was too curious to be hungry.

"Were you always this pretty?" Claire asked. "I mean, were you a really pretty boy?"

Natalie cocked one eyebrow at Claire. "I was never a boy," she said. Claire blushed, but Natalie went on talking. "I look like my baby pictures. When I hit puberty, I really started looking like a guy. You might not recognize a picture of me if you didn't know."

"Your makeup is amazing," I said because it was true, but also to give Claire a moment to recover.

"Years of practice," Natalie said with a grin.

"I'm sorry," Claire started, but Natalie waved a hand to stop her.

"You're going to slip up, it's natural. You've been really cool to Emily, and I know your heart's in the right place, so don't worry about it. Do you want to catch a movie? *Cloverfield* is starting in about twenty minutes."

"Oh I totally want to see that," Claire said and I agreed.

Natalie paid for the pizza, though I tried to protest, and we were off. I watched her walk and smiled more. Sure her hips were a little narrow, but she looked great. There might be hope for me after all—the faint flickering glimmer of hope that lay on the far side of having to talk to my parents. Could I get on hormones without their permission? A bitter taste flooded my mouth. The answer was as close as Natalie walking two steps in front of me and still impossibly far away.

CHAPTER NINE

CLAIRE

She was glad of the darkness in the theater so she could collect her thoughts. She didn't want it to bother her, but there was something about the way Natalie sounded so cavalier about surgeries and sex changes. There were only a few things in her life that Claire hadn't gotten around to questioning, but sex and how bodies were made was one of them.

And she liked Chris's body. He was a cute guy. Except for the girl-brain part. He looked great in sweaters because of his swimmer's shoulders, and she loved the feel of his hard chest and strong arms. Now he wanted to go and change everything. Was he going to grow breasts and have long hair and paint his nails? Wouldn't he just look like her boyfriend in drag?

Probably not, she had to admit after looking at Natalie for most of lunch. She might not know all the details, but she could see that the medical stuff they did to Natalie had worked. She had kind of a big jaw, but not bigger than a few of the girls at school. Claire knew plenty of girls who were taller than Natalie, and a few that were taller than Chris.

When she and Chris started going out last summer, she always assumed he would dump her someday for a prettier girl, not that he would want to *become* a prettier girl. The thought made her giggle and she put her hands over her mouth.

They'd met in a two-day poetry workshop offered by a visiting teacher from the Cities over a weekend. After the first day he came up and told her he really liked what she wrote, and how could she resist him after that? Besides, they liked a lot of the same things: music, computers, computer games, books, each other, and Chris even admitted to talking to God from time to time, but not in some weird super-religious way, which Claire thought was an adorable footnote to add to every other good quality about him. They'd been dating almost eight months. Chris was already her best friend and she felt like she'd known him most of her life—only to find she didn't know him that well at all.

She felt a little jealous of Natalie. Not that Chris was going to run off with her or something, just that she so clearly had what he needed right now.

And then there was that dizzy feeling, like the seat was going to fall away from under her at any moment. Men didn't just turn into women, and yet here in the theater, two seats away, was very distinctly a girl who had been born a boy. And, if Claire understood correctly, had at least one very boy part on her still. She couldn't help but think about it. What would it be like to go to school and have to hide that? Natalie couldn't change in the locker room, that was for sure. What happened if someone found out? She didn't know about Minneapolis, but out in Liberty lesser infractions than that sent people to the hospital. Some of the Neanderthals at school still thought it was sporting to "roll fags."

Off balance as she felt, she also had a strong wave of protectiveness welling up in her. Chris had stepped in and stopped other kids at school from calling her "death freak" or worse for wearing all black. Just dating him improved her social standing immensely, which meant almost no taunting anymore and occasionally an invite to a cool party. Not that she cared about those and she'd lose all of that if anyone found out about this transsexual stuff, but he'd lose a lot more. No matter what happened, she wouldn't let any harm come to Chris if she could stop it.

When the movie ended, Claire realized she'd paid scant attention to it. It was only six and they had another hour to play with before they had to drive back and assure their parents that the big city hadn't corrupted them.

"Come on," Natalie said. "Let's go shopping. What've you got for girl clothes?"

Chris blinked a couple times, looked over at her and then said, "Two sweaters, a pair of jeans and a skirt."

"What?" Claire asked before she could stop herself. "You have girl clothes? Do your parents know?"

He blushed. "They're in a duffel in my car with your name on it."

She laughed. "Oh. Cute. They're like ten sizes too big."

"They'll never notice."

"No pants?" Natalie cut in. "You need a good pair of dress pants. Come on."

She dragged them into Banana Republic and in a matter of minutes collected an armful of pants. Then she dragged the three of them into the large, handicap dressing room stall. "I need my boyfriend's opinion," she told the startled attendant and shut the door firmly, pushing the pants at Chris. "Brown first," she whispered.

Claire sat on the chair in the dressing room and watched with amazement. Natalie had plastered herself across the door and after a moment's pause, Chris pulled off his jeans and stepped into the pants, turning away momentarily to tuck himself so he'd fit into girls' pants. Claire forced herself not to look at Natalie and wonder what she did with her…Don't think of that, she told herself.

It wasn't the fit of the pants Claire saw when she turned her eyes from Natalie back to Chris, it was Chris's face. As the pants were zipped and buttoned and he turned to show them off, his face lightened. Most of the time his eyes were dark, haunted, and looked as if he was staring out of them from far away inside himself. Now they sparkled. It was like sitting in a dark room for months and then suddenly having the sun fall through an open window.

"Wow," she said.

"Do they look good?" Natalie asked because Chris couldn't voice the question. If the attendant was lurking outside, they needed it to sound like Natalie was showing off the pants, not Chris.

Claire stood up and touched Chris's cheek. "You look really happy," she said almost in a whisper. "I never saw how very sad you look all the time. I just thought that was how you looked, but this…this is you, happy."

Chris smiled, eyes bright with joy.

"I think I should get these pants," Natalie said loudly enough for the attendant to hear and winked at Chris.

Chris tried on the next pair, while Natalie talked quietly to Claire. "My mom said something similar when I started going to school like this. She said she'd been really worried about me and suddenly I was full of confidence and optimism. I told her I'd always been like that, I'd just spent so much energy fighting against that other thing that I had nothing left over."

None of the other pairs of pants worked as well as that first chocolate brown pair. When Chris was back in jeans, Natalie took the brown pants and went to the register. Chris offered to pay her back when they left the store, but she insisted it was a gift.

They said goodbye in the theater lobby with hugs all around. Claire tried not to pay attention to Natalie's breasts during the hug, but she couldn't help it. They felt very real, and she smelled like clover and oranges. It felt like hugging any other girl.

All the way back to Liberty, Claire watched Chris's face. It was like the sun coming out from behind clouds. She wanted to find a more unusual metaphor, but none came to mind. She just knew she'd never seen anything like it in her life. The closest was her mom the year after Dad left. She'd turned dark for a while, but mostly that was because she literally never opened the shades of the house to try and lift her mood. And then slowly, day by day, she went from being shadowed to the life-giving color Claire remembered. Even that wasn't as dramatic a change as she'd seen in Chris.

"You look good happy," she said.

"Is it really that obvious?"

"More than obvious."

She kissed Chris in the car and held tight to that newly alien, newly bright body for a few minutes. Then back through the snow to her living room where Mom was watching TV as usual.

"How was the city?" Mom asked as she paused the episode of *Bones* that she'd recorded.

"Great. Really fun." Claire dropped onto the couch. "We went to a big mall for pizza and a movie. What about your day? I thought you had a dinner date tonight."

"Are you trying to get me out of the house?"

Claire laughed. "If I wanted to see more of Chris, I'd just have him sneak in the window," she said.

"You're kidding, right? I hope you're kidding."

"Mom. Really."

"My date turned out to be a typical Aquarius," Mom said with a sigh.

"I told you those air signs are trouble for you."

Mom shook her head but she was smiling. She hit play and they watched to the next commercial. While her mom was fast forwarding through it, Claire asked, "What are you doing tomorrow?"

"Cleaning and I hope you are too, why?"

"Can we go shopping for non-black makeup? I think it's time for me to learn how to wear it."

Her mom grinned. She'd been trying to get Claire interested in cosmetics for the last year, especially since the lesbian jokes had started.

"Sure honey."

Claire smiled and settled back into the couch. If her mom knew what she was really going to use the cosmetics for it would probably fry her brain, but let her be happy about it instead. Everyone deserved to be happy.

CHAPTER TEN

Saturday night I watched a stupid kids' movie with Mikey, but I wasn't really watching the movie. I just took the opportunity of sitting still on the couch to replay the afternoon with Natalie and Claire over and over again. I fell asleep later still thinking about what Claire said about me looking happy. I hadn't known it was that obvious, but I did change that afternoon. No, "change" wasn't the right word. That would mean I'd become something else. It was more like I relaxed into me.

There had been so many years of pretense that I guess I didn't realize how different it made me to always be pretending. The trappings of boyhood were wrapped around me in layers, like wearing all my winter clothes, one sweater on top of another and then the jacket and scarf, in the middle of summer. Everyone was so used to seeing me as a mummy, they didn't know I could be any other way.

I'd learned to disconnect my ears and mouth from the rest of me so that I could hear all those words "son," "boy," "he/him" without them taking a chunk out of my soul every time. But what did that make me?

I wanted to live a real life. If magic didn't turn me into a real girl, the way I'd wanted as a kid, there were other ways. Natalie had done it, and now she went to school every day like I did, but she got to be herself, fully herself. I fell asleep wondering what that might be like.

In the morning, still in the T-shirt and boxers I slept in, I silently locked my door and then sat down at the computer to start my next phase of research. I'd seen a lot of these sites in the last couple years as I was still figuring things out, but now I looked in earnest, read deeply and made cryptic notes in my science notebook. There was one site that had a list called "Things you can do before your parents know." A few of those I was already doing, like performing well in school, saving money and researching my options. I already had my name picked out, but I hadn't started working on my voice. I resolved to start that next.

This summer would be the perfect time to practice my voice. I could download a few tracks to my iPod and rename them as exercises from a drama class I took last year. The iPod was another device my parents had no idea how to use, but even if they did snoop, they'd see the names and never give it a second thought. Then I could take it with me and practice in my car when I was alone.

The list also said I should take care of my skin, though there was no way with Dad and Mikey in the house that that was going to happen. They'd spot an exfoliant in the "men's bathroom" in a hot second. Mom had long ago taken over the master bathroom as her sanctuary and I could sometimes sneak in there, but not often enough. Maybe Claire would let me keep some skin products at her house.

Next I had to figure out how to get hormones. My mom was too young to start menopause, so I wasn't going to be able to sneak any estrogen replacement therapy from her assuming she even used it. I laughed. How many teenage kids sat around thinking about their mom's menopause? It was possible to illegally order hormones from an overseas pharmacy. But first there was that whole illegal issue, and I'd have to be sure of the quality and safety of them, plus where could I have them sent? I'd have to work on that. Plus there was electrolysis...I was going to need to make a lot more money.

Okay, that was the plan. This summer I would work on my voice and skin, while making as much money as humanly possible. The tip sheet also said it would be good to talk to a therapist, but I still thought Dr. Webber was not my guy. I'd try some hints in the next session because you never know. Speaking of hints, I wondered what my parents were doing today. Maybe I could start to see if Mom was at all receptive to the idea of having a daughter.

I unlocked my door, showered and threw on a weekend outfit: jeans, T-shirt, sweatshirt. Mom was in the living room reading the Sunday paper, and I could hear clattering sounds from the garage.

"You're finally up," Mom said, talking across the hall to me while I poured a bowl of cereal.

I glanced at the clock. It was almost eleven. "Yeah, I guess I'm catching up on my sleep."

"Do you really have that much homework?" she asked.

I took my bowl of cereal into the living room and sat on the other end of the couch from her, stretching my huge feet out on the coffee table. In Claire's house, no one ever rested their feet on the coffee table, but here it was impossible to keep Dad from doing it, and generally if Dad did it, Mikey and I could get away with it.

I shrugged while I swallowed a few bites. "It's not that much,"

I said. "I do some extra stuff, you know, for college and that. And sometimes I just get interested in something and stay up."

She smiled. "I used to stay up half the night reading when I was your age." That only enforced my belief that Mom was a lot smarter than she let on. She never went to college because she got pregnant in the last year of high school and married my dad. Sometimes I joked that she and I could go to college together, but she ignored that. I think she'd given up. At best she said she'd take some classes after she retired.

It was easy to forget how young my mom was. In another year, I'd be the same age she was when she had me. She actually looked youngest when she dressed up for work and blew her hair dry so that it feathered back in waves from her face. When she wasn't bustling around the house with her hair rough and her face scrunched in a look of disapproval, she was actually prettier than Claire's mom.

"Mom, do you ever wish you had a daughter?"

She put down her book. "Sometimes," she said. "I thought about getting pregnant again after Mikey. I love both of you, you know that right?"

"Sure, yeah."

"What are you worried about?" she asked. "I know you're not as masculine as your father, but you've become a wonderful young man."

"It's not that. I'm not worried about not being masculine," I said.

Her face hardened and she sat up. "Chris, I know your father and I don't take you to church every weekend, but we are good Christians and we don't support alternative lifestyles. You do understand that, don't you? If you have questions, you should talk to the doctor about that and get help."

My heart shriveled into a small, dark mass and then crumbled. If she was going to freak like that at the idea that I could be gay, there was no way I was getting anywhere with the "I'm really a girl" conversation.

"It's fine, Mom, it's not that. I like girls, really."

She smiled, though the gesture looked forced.

"Are Dad and Mikey in the garage?" I asked, standing up. She nodded. I put my bowl in the sink, washing the uneaten cereal down the drain. "I'm going to go bang on the car with them. Yell if Claire calls."

"Okay," she said.

I thought that would be the end of it, but it wasn't. You know what they say about adding insult to injury? Well, that came later in the evening. I worked on the Bronco with Dad and Mikey most of the afternoon. Showered again. Did some homework.

Dad knocked on my door after dinner, which was weird enough. I glanced toward the foot of the bed to make sure that "Claire's" duffel was in my car, which it was.

"Come in," I said.

He was already halfway through the door, but he shut it behind him, which was unusual. He sat down on my bed.

"Son," he said. "Your mother told me you were asking some questions this morning."

"Yeah," I said carefully neutral while the ice of panic dripped down the inside of my ribs.

"Were you afraid to talk to me?" he asked.

I thought, *About having a daughter? Yeah.* "Um, I guess," I managed. Could he possibly have figured it out? Or did they still think I was gay? "I'm not gay," I said.

He smiled thinly. "Of course you aren't. These kinds of things can happen to anyone."

Okay, he definitely had something in mind, but was he thinking what I was thinking? "So you know someone else with my...situation?" I asked. I felt like I was on some perverse game show where the loser is just taken out back and shot.

"Oh yeah, some of the guys I work with. You know, it's natural to go through this."

Now I knew we were not on the same page. But what page was he on? "What did they do?" I asked.

"Well, you should make sure you're taking your vitamins and eating well. And your mother thinks you're not sleeping enough.

Try not to be so uptight all the time, and don't...ah...take too many solo flights, if you get my drift."

Suddenly I was in that *Star Trek* episode where Picard cannot, for the life of him, figure out what the alien captain is saying because that race speaks entirely in metaphor, and yet they're supposed to fight a monster together. Vitamins? Solo flights?

He went on. "You tell Claire it's normal, and I'm sure she'll understand."

"She's fine about it, Dad."

"That's good. If it doesn't clear up in a few weeks, you come talk to me and we'll take you to a real doctor." He paused. "It still works some, right?"

I looked at him blankly.

"You can get it up some of the time, right? And you're not having trouble peeing or anything like that?"

My face turned redder than Mars. I wanted to burst out laughing and crying. He thought I was having trouble with impotence. Good Lord!

"No, Dad," I managed, barely remembering the question he just asked. "It's probably just the late nights and stress."

He stood up and clapped his hand on my shoulder. "That's my boy. Don't be afraid to talk to me."

"Sure," I said, holding my breath until he was safely out of the door.

The room felt too small and closing in even further, but where could I go? It was February, I couldn't just take a walk. No stores were open on Sunday night. I swore soundlessly for a few minutes and then put my face in my hands. I try to talk to my parents about transsexualism and they think I'm impotent.

Well, I thought, *it's in the ballpark*. I still wanted to put my fist through the wall.

I carefully went downstairs saying to Mom, "Books are in my car" and then continued on blessedly outside into the frigid night. The icy air helped. I'd left my scarf inside and kept my jacket unzipped, standing out by my car, staring up at the sky until the tips of my fingers started to go numb.

***

After school on Monday, Claire had one of her bazillion clubs and Tuesday I had a short off-season swim training, so it was Wednesday before I could tell her about the totally bizarre conversation with Dad. She literally fell off the bed laughing.

"Impotent," she gasped from the floor. "Oh, that's rich."

"Sometimes I wish I was," I admitted.

She pushed up on her elbows. "Well I don't. I like your…boy parts."

"Thanks, I think."

"Oh don't mope," she said, picking herself up and sitting back on the bed. "I got you something."

"What?" I asked, thinking it was a new computer game or a book.

She opened her closet and pulled out a small black satchel, handing it to me. I unzipped it. There was liquid foundation, a compact with four shades of eye shadow, a bunch of brushes to put it on with, bronzer, an eyebrow pencil, two lipsticks and mascara. I must have looked at her blankly, because she sat down looking concerned.

"Is it okay? I told Mom I wanted makeup, so some of it might be the wrong colors, but I can show you how to do the eyes, I think. I'm sorry, I've avoided my mom's crazy ideas of womanhood so long that I missed a few lessons in all this stuff."

I grabbed her and hugged her until she grumbled, "You're crushing me."

"It's the best," I told her.

She shut the door and locked it. "Here are the makeup removing wipes. Mom isn't supposed to get home for a couple hours, but if she does, I'll go distract her while you get it off, okay?"

I nodded.

"All right, hold still." She took the foundation out of the bag and a triangular sponge. "Man, this is weird."

"If you don't want to—" I started.

"Shut up," she said. "Just let me be weirded out, okay?"

I looked at her closely, but she was smiling a little, so I let it go.

We played around for about an hour, and I turned out to be better with the eye makeup than Claire. "You are so doing my makeup for prom," she quipped. At the end of it, I looked okay. Slightly drag queenish because we overdid the eye color and Claire put the blush too low, but on the whole, very good for a first try. I was going to have to figure out some reason to pluck my eyebrows. Maybe I could audition for the school play; that would give me a good cover story.

I looked at myself in the mirror for a while, trying to figure out where I could get a wig. Natalie would know. Then I wiped it all off, using three wet wipes to make sure I got every last trace.

"Thanks," I told Claire.

I flopped down on the bed on my back and held my arms open to her. She cuddled up to me and propped herself up on her elbow so she was looking down into my face.

"Don't mention it," she said. "Is it okay if I still think you're cuter without makeup?"

"I guess, I kind of still have a guy face."

"You should try guyliner sometime."

"What?" I asked.

"You know, when guys in the movies wear dark eyeliner and it makes their eyes look really sexy."

"But—" I started.

"I know," she said. "You're not a guy. But if you ever get busted, tell them you were going for the guyliner look."

I grinned up at her and wondered if she would think it was too weird for us to kiss after I'd been wearing makeup. I didn't get to find out because we heard her mom coming in the front door and she sat up quickly on the bed. "That's your cue," she said, giving me a quick kiss. "See you tomorrow."

"Bye, Ms. Davis," I said to Claire's mom as I was heading for the door.

She turned from the counter where she'd set her purse. "Hi Chris, you don't want to stay and catch *NCIS*? There's a gothic woman in it, like Claire."

From the doorway to her room, Claire rolled her eyes at me, though we did both agree that the character of Abby on *NCIS* was awesome. The issue was her mother's attempts to be friendly. Claire thought it was bad enough that her mom was more like a sister to her. She didn't want the three of us to pal around together, even on the couch in the privacy of her own home.

"Thank you, but I've got to get working on my homework," I said and slipped into the cold air.

I drove home and checked myself in the rearview mirror one more time to make sure I had no lingering eyeliner. I felt a little stupid to be so jazzed about makeup. The guys at school would totally kick my ass if they knew. But on the other hand, I looked better than some of the girls who went crazy with makeup and huge hair. I had to figure out how to look less like a drag queen, though. If only I had a sister whose fashion magazines I could steal. I'd have to find good makeup tips from the Internet.

CHAPTER ELEVEN

CLAIRE

She cleaned up the compacts, bottles and jars scattered across her bed. She'd put on light eyeshadow too so she could tell her mother she was just showing her boyfriend her new makeup. Mom was delighted, but Claire was feeling more than a little freaked out as she wiped the makeup off after two hours of *NCIS*.

The first problem was that he actually looked good with makeup—and not just George Clooney with eyeliner good. In part it was the way Chris's whole self brightened around girl stuff, and the fact that his deep set brown eyes really came out with a good application of color. And he was better at putting it on than she was, which embarrassed her, though she'd spent a few years deliberately screwing up any non-black makeup so Mom wouldn't make her wear it. When she had to wear it, it just felt oppressive. She didn't think girls should have to paint themselves to look pretty.

Too bad she and Chris couldn't just swap bodies. Not that she wanted to be a boy. She liked the whole girl thing, just not the übergirl activities that her mom went in for, manicures and that stuff. But she liked being able to cry at movies and the feeling of being held by someone bigger than her. She really liked that part, and she and Chris hadn't done as much of it since he started talking about being Emily. Come to think of it, she'd spent more time holding him lately. Tonight was the first time in weeks she'd curled up under his arm.

"What were you thinking?" she asked in the general direction of up. "You couldn't just keep the girls in the girls' bodies? Aren't giraffes weird enough?"

She didn't get a direct reply, but she did feel a vast patience settling down on her as she often did when she asked something ridiculous.

"I guess I'm still scared," she said more calmly. "Like what if that happened to me? And what's Chris going to do? And what... what are people going to think about me because I love a freak?"

She paused. "I don't really mean it like that. He's not a freak. Not much anyway. I mean not any more than half the kids at school, the Future Farmers of America and all that. I don't know what you were thinking with those kids either."

She felt smiled upon. At least God had a sense of humor. Claire reached for her Bible and let it fall open. She probably shouldn't dog the FFA kids when she consulted her Bible on a regular basis.

It opened to the Song of Solomon, chapter three: "On my bed by night I sought him whom my soul loves; I sought him, but found him not. I will rise now and go about the city, in the streets and in the squares; I will seek him whom my soul loves."

Her Bible study group had a guest speaker last summer who

talked about how the Song of Solomon was a metaphor for the love affair between the soul and God. "Him whom my soul loves" could refer to God, Himself.

"It's just another way to find You," she said, mostly to herself since God already knew. "You want us to keep discovering You, and this whole thing with Chris, it's another way to have faith in You, to see You in the world no matter how crazy it looks at first."

There was something St. John of the Cross said in a poem he wrote. She pulled the book off her bookshelf and thumbed through to the poem entitled "A Vital Truth." There was the line: "An altar is every pore and every hair on every body—confess that, dear God, confess."

That included Chris's body. People liked to think that life was so stable, even her with her own pretensions of being holier than thou and oh so open-minded. But God's plan wasn't the same as the things we all made up day-to-day, she thought. What was the saying? "Men plan, God laughs."

She curled up in bed to read the whole Song of Solomon. The dialogue between two lovers was one of her favorite parts of the Bible. It echoed the longing she felt for God sometimes. She might not have any person she could talk to about the situation with Chris, but she could talk to God and as strange as it seemed, she understood that God knew what He was doing.

CHAPTER TWELVE

After the evening at Claire's house playing with makeup, I figured it was time to tackle the psych class assignment. I sat down at the computer, opened a new file and stared at it. I couldn't say any of the things that came to mind.

What would I do if I woke up tomorrow as a girl? I'd cry for joy, to start. Then I'd run around and show myself off to everyone. I'd make Mom take me shopping for all new clothes, and I'd grow my hair long. I'd probably still swim; it makes me feel good and it would keep me in shape. The girls who swim have really nice bodies. I wonder if I'd still be this tall. If I could pick it, I'd be a few inches shorter with B-cup breasts, nothing too outrageous, and hips like Mom's, kind of solid-looking.

While I was thinking, I opened GenderPeace in my browser and sent a note to Natalie, asking where I could get hormones. I reflexively glanced over my shoulder, but my bedroom door was solidly closed. Since meeting Natalie I felt bolder, but I didn't want to get careless. Message sent, I closed that window and stared at the blank page again.

This was going to take all night. I heard Mikey coming up the stairs and yelled, "Hey, come here?"

He stuck his head in my room, "What?"

"I have to do this lame thing for psych class. What would you do if you woke up tomorrow as a girl?"

"Gross," he said. "I'd stay home."

He pushed himself out of the doorway and into the bathroom. Well, that was a start. I wrote:

"If I woke up as a girl, I'd stay home and play video games. If it didn't go away, I'd call the doctor. If I had to go out, I'd go to another city where no one would recognize me."

That was so stupid I had to stop writing. I went down a few lines and tried again, reversing it:

"If I woke up as a boy I'd pretend everything was normal and go to school as usual. No one would know what happened and they'd be afraid to ask me about it, so I could pretty much go through my life as usual. They would wonder what had happened and if I was okay, but they wouldn't know how to talk about it with me and I'd use that to my advantage. I would pretend it didn't really matter to me what they thought, even if it did.

"Over time I'd start to get good at pretending, and people would forget that I'd been different. They'd just go by what they saw and treat me like a boy and after a while I'd wonder if I'd really been a girl at all. I'd start to think I was supposed to be a boy, even if I felt like a girl on the inside."

Slightly better. I went back and changed "boy" to "girl" and vice versa. Then I went to bed.

I dreamed that it was Sunday morning again and I woke up

with a girl's body. In the dream, I got up and showered for the longest time. No one treated me any differently, except Claire who said I looked really cute.

***

It was Thursday and time for another session with Dr. No. I'd been dreading this stupid appointment all day. I didn't want to talk about my childhood or my dad, so I figured I'd bring up something I really did want to know about. I dropped down on the couch and watched Dr. Webber settle into his seat, notepad in his lap.

"What would you like to talk about today, Chris?" he asked.

"What do you know about transsexualism?" I asked. I figured what the hell, I could always say I was joking, and I was sick of screwing around with this goon.

He scribbled in his notepad and then looked up. "It's a very rare condition," he said. "Do you like dressing up in women's clothing? Does it turn you on?"

Not when you put it like that, I thought. Gross. "No," I said.

"You know what I think," he said, leaning forward in a conspiratorial way. "I think you're afraid of growing up like your father. You may have fantasies of being a woman because you think that's the only way to avoid being like him. Let's come up with some other options, okay?"

"Sure," I said.

I should have known he'd be able to put a really crazy spin on this, but it still caught me off guard and shut me up again.

"Who are some other men you can think of?" he asked. "Men you could be like when you grow up?"

Natalie, I thought, or any of a dozen people I'd met on GenderPeace. Or Tammy Baldwin, the State Rep. from Wisconsin who had the guts to be an out lesbian in the U.S. Congress, she was great. Or any woman politician or scientist or those running big technology companies...Oh, right, those aren't men—they were just the people I wanted to be like when I grew up. Think.

How about Joan Roughgarden the biologist? I'd loved reading *Evolution's Rainbow* and learning about how diverse sexuality and gender could be on our planet. Or maybe Susan Kimberly, the former St. Paul City Council member who publicly transitioned and went right back to being in politics? Nope, being born with a male body and having the guts to transition to be yourself wasn't going to count for Dr. Webber's "men you could be like" quiz.

"Mr. Cooper, my psych teacher, he's cool," I said, thinking, *crap, that assignment is due tomorrow.*

"What do you like about him?"

This was the stupidest game, but I had to go on playing it for the next forty minutes. "He's smart and educated and he usually *listens* to the students." That last part was thrown in for Dr. Webber's benefit, but he didn't seem to get the hint.

"Good, Chris, so you'd like to be a man who is smart and educated. Do you want children?"

I shrugged. "Maybe." I looked at the clock on the wall. What I wanted was to carry my own children...I couldn't even stand to think about it in front of this jerk. I stood up and paced across the room.

"You're afraid if you have children, you'll hurt them, aren't you?"

"Sure," I said, thinking, *You absolute dumb ass.* I didn't want to talk about children, so I went back to brainstorming other male role models and letting him pick out the qualities of the man he thought I should grow into.

In the car with Mom on the way home I told her, "I don't want to go to Dr. Webber anymore. It's not helping."

"But you seem happier," she said.

I hadn't thought about the effect that talking to Claire and meeting Natalie had on me, and that Mom connected that positivity to me seeing the shrink. Damn. I'd have to go again. Maybe I could fake an illness next Thursday.

At home I automated my dinner table conversation.

/run: dinner with the family
1. smile
2. listen politely
3. look bored appropriate to normal teenager
4. talk about math class
5. ask Dad about the Bronco
6. smile
7. get Mikey talking about comic books
8. exit

As soon as I could excuse myself, I did so, saying I had to finish my psych paper. I pulled out a notebook and a pen and wrote so hard the tip tore through the paper in places:

"If I woke up as a girl I'd have my own kids, and I'd let them grow up to be whatever they wanted. I'd get pregnant and carry them in my own body. I'd get a period like a normal girl. I'd be able to go through labor and nurse my own babies. I'd be able to be a mother."

At that point I was crying so hard I couldn't write anymore. I tore the sheet out of the notebook and ripped it up until I couldn't make the pieces any smaller. Then I threw the notebook across the room and crawled into bed, curling up as small as possible and crying myself to sleep.

***

On Friday I turned in an essay to psych class that bore no resemblance to what I'd written the night before. Afterward, Claire told me that her mom was out on a date again and did I want to come over? I didn't know what I wanted to do. I felt like I could sleep for a week.

"Sure," I said.

"You look like crap," she told me while we were eating a pizza in front of the TV. "What happened?"

"A bunch of stuff. Stupid Dr. Webber...and I have to keep

going because Mom thinks that's making me happier, and then that dumb psych assignment. What if I woke up as a girl? Geez."

"Harsh," Claire said. "You know what you need?"

"What?" I mumbled, thinking that if she wanted to make out for a while I could probably pull it off. The physical contact would do me good.

"A hot bath."

"For real?"

"Totally."

When we finished the pizza and *NCIS*, she started filling the tub and dumped in some bath salts.

"Take as long as you want," she said. "You can use my stuff if you want. I'll be gaming. Vaorlea the Mighty is close to leveling, and then I can finally get out of that stupid zone."

"This whole bath thing is just so I'll leave you alone so you can game, isn't it?" I asked. It wasn't a serious question because Claire had plenty of gaming time anyway. Her mom always assumed that being alone in her bedroom meant she was reading or doing homework.

"Whatever you say, honey," she said with a wink as she closed the bathroom door behind her. She was too sweet.

I shucked my clothes and lowered myself into the steaming water. I took baths sometimes when I could get the house to myself. Mom's bathroom was the only one with a tub, and I was afraid I'd give myself away if I took too many lingering baths. Plus at my house we didn't have all this cool stuff: exfoliating facial scrub, a loofah, bath salts.

I soaked for a while and then took up Claire's razor to do away with the new growth of fuzz on my arms and legs. If I could have thought of a good cover story, I might have stopped shaving my arms, but since the going belief was that I shaved everything to cut drag in the water, I had to keep it all up or let it all go, and I wasn't going to let that hair grow back on my legs or my chest. Most of the swim team guys stopped shaving when the season ended. Okay, except for me they all did. But they left me alone about it.

All smooth, I drained out the hairy, dirty water and filled the tub again with clean, hot water. I put my head back and soaked longer. Then I tucked what Claire calls my "boy parts" down between my legs and had a good look at myself in the water.

Yeah, I looked like a boy all right, but if I squinted a little I saw how I could have looked. I had good long legs and, if I kept weight off, a flat stomach. Still no waist to speak of. Claire had this cute little waist that I could almost wrap my hands around, which made me feel monstrous. I wondered if she'd trade my waist for hers.

She tapped on the door. "Hey Little Mermaid, how's it going?"

I untucked and sat up a little. "Come on in."

She opened the door and stuck her head in. "I just wanted to warn you that we're approaching the earliest time Mom could return home if the date wasn't that interesting."

"Oh thanks." I opened the drain and let the water start to run out.

"You look cute," Claire added and closed the door again.

A few times in the past, she'd climbed into the tub with me, and I wondered why she didn't now. Probably because her mom could come home, but it worried me a little bit. She still kissed me and touched me in that slightly possessive girlfriend way when we hung out together, but she hadn't tried to initiate anything longer or more intimate.

Before I came out to her, we'd make out at least once a week and if we knew we had an evening to ourselves, go further than that. She seemed to really like kissing and wasn't that self-conscious about taking her clothes off. Often she'd end up mostly undressed and somehow I'd still have my jeans on. It was easier to be sexual without the constant reminder that my body wasn't right.

And Claire had rarely pushed me about that even though she usually initiated our times together. I wondered if she'd thought I was pathologically shy about my boy parts or how she'd explained that to herself and now that I thought about it, that was a pretty good explanation. In the last few weeks, she hadn't really tried anything—not since that night she hopped into my lap when I was trying to come out to her.

What would happen to us if she wasn't attracted to me anymore? I was already cold when I stood up from the bath and toweled off quickly. She never would have just put me in the bath by myself before.

I pulled on my clothes and left the bathroom intending to ask her. She was on the couch with another episode of *NCIS* cued up and a bowl of popcorn. She patted the seat next to her and my momentum dissolved. I didn't want to have a long emotional talk about our relationship. This was comfortable.

When I sat next to her, she put the popcorn bowl in my lap and leaned against my shoulder. I looked down at the top of her black hair and wondered, *Was our relationship changing as I changed?*

***

The first sign of a bad week was that I got my psych paper back on Tuesday with a "C" on it and a note that said "See me." I thought about bolting for my car again, but this meeting was going to be inevitable. I waited until the end of the day, so there wouldn't be other students around in case Mr. Cooper was going to say something really embarrassing.

He sat at his desk sorting papers, so I knocked on the open door. He looked up and ran a hand through his hair, which made it messier. Pink windburn still shone on his cheeks and two of the knuckles on his right hand were cracked from dryness. I didn't know his story, but he was clearly not from Minnesota. If I hadn't been freaked out about the paper assignment, I'd have recommended he get some Corn Huskers lotion like Dad used.

"Ah, Chris, come on in. I thought you might be avoiding me."

I stepped up to the front of the desk. "You wanted to see me."

"About your paper. I was surprised. It showed a real lack of imagination," he said. He tapped the paper in front of him with a long, blunt finger even though it wasn't mine. "That's not like you. And the end was pretty dark. Do you have a problem with women?"

"No," I said.

"But you can't imagine yourself as a woman." It was a question delivered as a statement.

I shrugged.

He picked up another stack of papers and thumbed through them until he found mine and read a few sentences silently to himself.

"This end here. It sounds like you think that no one notices you. Do you struggle with low self-esteem?"

I shrugged again.

"Chris," he said. "You're one of my smarter students. You have the potential to be really good with people. If there's something bothering you or you're in some kind of trouble at home…"

"Mom has me seeing a shrink," I said. "And I've been doing better the last couple of weeks."

"Good, good. Now, do the paper over again and apply yourself, and let me know if there's anything else you need."

He stood up and held out his hand to shake. He was taller than me by a couple inches, which I didn't notice when I was in my seat. I thought we were the same height.

"Lotion," I told him.

"What?"

"Your knuckle is bleeding."

While he was looking at the back of his hand, I backed out the door. Do the paper again? He had to be kidding me. I wasn't one for cheating, but this was one assignment I was going to hand over to Claire wholesale. She'd swap me for help on her geometry homework.

If I hadn't been so rattled by the thing with Mr. Cooper on Tuesday I might have checked my psych class schedule and realized that I'd planned to skip Wednesday's class altogether.

It wasn't until I was in my seat that I realized I'd screwed up. This was the day we had the guest speakers from the Gay and Lesbian Action Council. As it turned out, we got one gay and one lesbian.

They had guts to drive out into the boonies and talk to a bunch of high school kids about "alternative lifestyles." Apparently they were also talking to a senior history class and someone's social studies class. We were right in the middle and our class was combined with a second history class, which was how another twenty students, including Claire, got crammed into our room. Like a secret agent, she winked at me and then sat down across the room and ignored me completely, earning my profound gratitude.

I already knew all sorts of stuff about being gay because a lot of the transgender resource pages I looked at were linked with gay and lesbian sites. Plus I liked girls, which meant I was going to end up as a lesbian at some point in my life. So I listened but practiced my totally bored look.

Most of the kids in the class had pretty boring questions, so the bored look wasn't hard to come by. "What do you think about the Bible's condemnation of homosexuality?" "Do you plan to have kids?" "Are you scared of getting AIDS?" "When did you know?" "How did you know?" etc.

The speakers were better than I expected. The woman was a marketing person for a big corporation, and the guy was a carpenter, which I thought was neat. Thank goodness he wasn't a hairstylist. He was awfully pretty for a carpenter, though; it might have been better if he hadn't cleaned up so well for this event. He had carefully combed, short shaggy hair that hung over his forehead and big, dark eyes along with a wide nose. He wore khakis and a button-down shirt, but no tie, and the woman wore gray slacks with a burgundy sweater that I wanted to touch to feel if it was as soft as it looked. Her black hair fell past her shoulders. I think someone at the Gay and Lesbian Action Center might have picked out a feminine lesbian and a butch gay man just to say *See, we're not all stereotypes.*

I listened more intently to the questions than the answers, because of the crucial importance of knowing my classmates' various stands on homosexuality, and by association, other variations having to do with gender.

"Don't you wish you'd just been born a woman?" one of the girls asked the man. I pushed my hands against my desk so I wouldn't lean forward.

"Not really," he said. "I have no desire to be a woman. Being attracted to men and being a woman are two very different things."

My face felt like the surface of the sun. I prayed it didn't look that red.

"I think your teacher has been talking to you about this," he said as he stood up and went for a piece of chalk. He wrote "sexual orientation" across the board and below it "gender identity."

"These are two different things and they don't go together. Sexual orientation is what makes you straight or gay. Gender identity is what has you be a man or a woman. Since I'm a man who is attracted to men, that makes me gay. If I was a man who felt he was really a woman that would make me transgender." He wrote "transgender" across the bottom of the board.

I prayed to die in an abrupt fashion like a heart attack or being hit by a meteor right then. I thought I wanted to know how my classmates felt, but now that it came down to it, I didn't. I'd take any random act of God to get me out of this class. At any moment I was sure every head in the room was going to turn and look at me, and the only thing that kept me in my seat was knowing that if I bolted for the door it would happen that much sooner.

"What?" some guy near the front asked. "What the hell is that?"

"Jason," Mr. Cooper said in a warning tone.

"It's okay," the gay guy said. "Transphobia is one of the last remaining prejudices that many people think is acceptable. While it's becoming more accepted to be gay and lesbian, and therefore less cool to be homophobic, a lot of people still react badly to transgender people—probably because of their own insecurities about sex and gender. 'Transgender' is an umbrella term that includes everything from men who like to dress up as women from time to time to people who actually go through a sex change operation, both male to female and female to male."

I was in a rictus of death prayer: take me now, take me now. Across the room, Claire's hand shot up.

"Yes?" Mr. Cooper sounded relieved to have someone to call on who wasn't a football guy.

"I don't think it's fair to put that all in one category," Claire said. "Do you really think someone who cross-dresses belongs in the same group as a person who is, say, a man trapped in a woman's body?"

"That's a great point," the lesbian said. "And there's a lot of debate going on in the LGBT—that's lesbian, gay bisexual and transgender—community about that. Some transsexuals don't even want to be associated with lesbians and gay men because they're heterosexual after transition and simply want to live a normal life."

"Whoa," said football guy Jason. "You're saying a guy can turn into a girl and live a normal life? That's fucked up."

"It is not!" Claire said too loudly. Everyone was staring at her now and I could only think, *Thank you Lord that isn't me.* "Transsexual people are just like you and me, they just have a much harder life. How would you feel if you knew you were really a girl trapped in that meathead body?"

"Like a pussy," he said and the class cracked up. Except for me; I couldn't move.

"Quiet down!" Mr. Cooper shouted. His face was really red now beyond the windburned spots and all the way up to his forehead.

"That's fucked up," Jason said again into the silence. He continued, "God didn't make gays, and he sure as hell didn't make men to wear dresses and want to be chicks. That's disgusting."

Mr. Cooper opened his mouth to shut Jason up, but before he could, a hurtling mass of bound paper smacked into the side of

Jason's head and knocked him out of his desk. He was on his feet in a second, Claire's offending history book in his hand, lunging toward her. Three other football guys grabbed him, while the two kids closest to Claire got hold of her arms.

She looked fantastic, all that dark hair flying around her head.

"You unholy, unwashed, blaspheming, heathen bastard, you think you know the will of God! How dare you!" she was screaming, followed by a string of fairly unChristian words.

My body got up without me and walked down to her. I thought I was still sitting in my seat, shaking, but the preprogrammed part that played her boyfriend day-to-day knew what to do at a time like this. My hand reached out for her shoulder. She stopped fighting and threw herself at me crying. *Well, at least one of us gets to cry*, I thought.

"Both of you, principal's office now!" Mr. Cooper shouted. He really was a lot taller than me when he stood up straight like that.

He closed his hand around Jason's arm and propelled him through the door into the hall. Claire followed, and I went with her.

CHAPTER THIRTEEN

In the hall outside the classroom, Mr. Cooper glanced at me. "You can come too," he said in a normal tone as he shifted his grip on Jason's arm and marshaled us all toward the end of the hall.

I ended up in the waiting area outside the principal's office with Jason while Mr. Cooper dragged Claire in to explain why she'd chucked her book at Jason. His eye was darkening where the corner of the book hit it. Okay, I told myself, time for an Oscar-winning performance playing guy-to-guy conversation so I could make sure Claire would be okay around him and the other football lunks.

Sprawled into the seat jock-style, I looked over at him. "Man, that's gonna be a shiner."

He touched it with his fingertips. "I've had worse."

"No shit," I said. "Sorry she went apeshit on you. She gets crazy sometimes. You know, girl stuff."

"Yeah?"

"Yeah." I took a deep breath. "Look, she may be a little nutty, but she's my girl, so if you're going to take it out on someone, come find me, okay?"

"Hey, I wouldn't hit a girl anyway," he said. "I just don't want a fucking suspension. Then I might come kick your ass." He was grinning as he said it, so I grinned back. He made a fist and slammed it into my shoulder. It hurt enough that I knew I'd have a good bruise, but things could have been so much worse that I didn't care.

"We're cool," he said. "As long as you keep her the hell away from me."

I nodded, trying to figure out if I was supposed to say something else. The principal's office door opened and Claire came out while Mr. Cooper waved Jason in.

Claire kept walking out of the administrative office, so I followed her.

"I'm sorry," she said.

"What? Did you—?" My blood froze.

"No," she said. "I didn't tell them anything. Can you drive me home?"

I was going to miss English again, but I'd survive. The teacher loved me, and I'd already done the homework for this month. "Yeah, what happened?"

"I'm suspended for a week."

"Crap."

"Yeah."

I caught up to her and put an arm around her shoulders. "You gave him a black eye, you know."

She shook her head, tears welling up in her eyes again. "I'm sorry. I hate to hurt anyone, but he was such a jackass." She tried to smile a little. "I told the principal and Mr. Cooper that I have a cousin who's transsexual and that it's really hard on her and we're close. I think they might think I was talking about myself, wouldn't that be funny."

"Funny," I said, deadpan. "I told Jason you were PMSing and that he could beat me up if he had a problem with you."

"You did not."

"Guy's honor," I said.

"Good Lord," she said. "We're too weird for this place. Take me home. I've got to figure out how to bribe Mom to lie about my 'cousin' if they call her."

***

I didn't mention to my folks about Claire's suspension, but I did send Natalie a note, and posted a long description of the incident on GenderPeace. Thursday at school was a bummer without her there, made worse by the recollection that I had to suffer through Dr. Webber again; he apparently had something going on in his personal life and his office called early in the week to move the appointment, for an hour later. Maybe we could talk about his issues for once instead of mine. I wasn't sure I could handle it with as harsh as the week felt already. Worst case, I'd just sit in his office and cry for fifty minutes.

At the appointed hour I sat with Mom in the dreaded waiting room, trying to come up with things I could say to kill an hour. Maybe I could pretend to have questions about being gay. Maybe we could just talk about schoolwork for an hour. Or I could talk about Claire and see if he'd give me more information about being a woman, that could be fun. Maybe I'd ask about PMS.

The person coming down the hall to the waiting room wasn't Dr. Webber, though. I thought she'd pass us by, but she came over to Mom and me. She looked like someone's grandmother with her short gray-black hair and a wide face. She held her hand out to my mom.

"Mrs. Hesse, I'm Dr. Mary Mendel. Dr. Webber has had a family emergency and I'm seeing some of his clients. Chris, would you like to talk to me today?"

"Sure," I said, though I didn't really care who I had to spend that time with. I knew there wasn't any other answer I could give in front of Mom and get away with it.

When I stood up, she only came to my midchest, even shorter than Claire.

Her office looked a lot like Dr. Webber's except it was more colorful, and in one corner she had a box of toys: stuffed animals and foam bats and funny shaped pillows.

"Do you see kids a lot?" I asked as I sat on the couch.

"Yes, and sometimes my adult clients like to play with the toys too." She smiled, crinkling her eyes. Her eyes were a clear blue like the January sky when it's too cold to snow but the sun still feels really warm on your skin. I liked her hair too because it was one of those I-don't-care-what-you-think short styles. It looked good on her because of her square face, but I got the impression that she picked it from a list of the most low maintenance styles possible.

She sat in a chair across from me and opened a manila file, scanning down the page. "So you've been here a few times, how has it been for you?"

"It's fine," I said. "Mom thinks it's making me happier."

She nodded. "You like to make the people around you happy, don't you?"

"Yeah."

"What makes you happy?"

I shrugged while I went through the long list of things I couldn't say. "I like to read, and hang out with my girlfriend Claire, she's cool. And she lets me play *World of Warcraft* on her computer, that's fun."

Dr. Mendel smiled, which made the corners of her eyes crinkle more. "What characters do you have?"

"Do you really want to know?" I asked. I didn't have the patience to bullshit about stuff I actually cared about. "I mean, do you know what kinds there are?"

"My grandkids taught me to play *Champions of Norrath* on their PlayStation," she explained. "Sometimes we play games as a family. I like the Cleric; isn't that funny for a therapist, so righteous?"

"Yeah," I agreed. "I've got a Mage, Amalia, she's my favorite, and a Priest. I like the magic-users."

"Because of the magic or the damage they can do?" she asked.

I sat up in the chair and really looked at her. She smiled back at me. She was serious, and she'd just asked me the smartest question I'd ever heard about gaming outside of the game itself.

"The magic," I said.

"I like characters that heal," she said. "I think you can tell a lot about what's important to someone by the kinds of characters they play. What's your Priest's name?"

"Thalia. They're both girls. Do you think that's weird?"

"No," she said. "Do you?"

"I don't know."

"Really?" she asked.

I'd evaded her question and we both knew it, but what was I going to say? Should I tell her it wasn't weird for me at all and often felt more real than my real life, at least the part about being female? I was not going to sit through another hour of hearing how I wanted to grow up differently from my father.

"Yeah, I think it's weird," I said. "But a lot of guys play female characters. They have nice butts."

She cocked her head to one side and looked at me. "And you're just like a lot of guys, are you?"

"No," I said really fast and then stopped myself.

She looked down at the folder in her hands again and traced down the page with one finger.

"Last time with Dr. Webber you brought up transsexualism. Were you trying to get a rise out of him?" she asked.

"Sure," I said.

Again, she looked at me for a long time without saying anything. I tried to look back at her, but I ended up picking at the seam of my jeans inside my knee.

Finally she asked, "'Sure' means 'I'm agreeing with you in order to make you happy,' doesn't it?"

I didn't know what to say, but I gave her a little nod.

"You weren't trying to be antagonistic, were you?" she asked.

She paused again and I nodded. I was so afraid and hopeful at the same time that I could feel tears pushing at the edge of my eyes. I blinked hard and let my eyes burn with the effort of not crying.

"I'm not crazy," I said.

"I don't think you are," she agreed. "Do you want to know how you look to me?"

"Yes."

"You look like someone who is very tense, very guarded. You have a lot of anger and grief, and some really strong defenses. You're also very sensitive, intelligent and caring. I'd like to see more of you come out." Dr. Mendel closed the folder and set it on the end table next to her. "I want you to know that anything you say in this room I will not repeat to your parents. No notes, no record, just a place for you to talk, okay?"

I wanted to tell her but I just couldn't.

After a moment of quiet, she went on. "I think if I had something that was very sensitive and I wanted help but was afraid to ask for it, that I might bring it up casually to see what response I got. If you had asked me what I thought about transsexualism I would tell you that I'm familiar with the standards of care detailed by the World Professional Association for Transgender Health and I do meet their guidelines for mental health professionals."

"You do?" the question jumped out of my mouth.

She nodded.

"Claire says when I'm…when I get to be a girl that I look happier." Just saying the words put a lump in my throat but lifted a huge weight off my chest. "But she and Natalie are the only two people who know. Other than you."

She smiled. "Chris—" she started, then paused. "That's not right is it? Do you have a name you call yourself?"

I didn't know if I had the guts to say it out loud in the middle of the day in the shrink's office, but my lips moved without me telling them to. "Emily," I whispered. "After my grandma."

"Emily, do you want me to transfer you into my care, so you can see me every week?"

"Totally!"

"Do you want to bring Claire with you next week?"

"Yes!"

"Good, I'll see you both then. I need to talk to your mother now about transferring you into my practice. I promise I won't tell her anything about what you said here today. I'm just going to tell her that I think you respond better to a woman doctor, and then I'm going to call in some favors with Webber so he won't argue. We should be all set."

"Man, she is so going to think I have it in for Dad," I said.

"We can work on strategies for relating to your parents," Dr. Mendel said. "And for coming out to them, but for right now I want you to know you're safe."

"Thanks," I told her. "That's…that's *great*."

***

The visit with Dr. Mendel gave me enough hope to coast through the following week. Claire had a rough time with her mom about school and ended up grounded, which I think meant that she spent all her time in her room reading and playing *World of Warcraft*. She could only talk to me on the phone for five minutes at a time, to get updates from school, but we sent each other long emails.

Her mom had tried to cut off Internet access, but Claire protested that she needed it to research the papers she was working on, which might have been true, but I think it was more to research having a higher level WoW character. I wondered if someday we could get Dr. Mendel into WoW with us when I wasn't her patient anymore. We already had one grandmother in our guild, and she was very sweet to everyone and always called me "honey" when we chatted.

Natalie invited me to meet her in the city on Sunday to go to a support group she had to attend, so off I went with a flimsy excuse to Dad about a pair of goggles I wanted to buy for swimming that I couldn't find in Liberty. The team still had off-season workouts twice a week, though missing one wasn't as big a deal as during the season. I usually went out of habit.

We met at a little brunch place and had a bite to eat before going to a stocky brick community center building. Inside it looked like a mutated school with long corridors branching off each other, filled with thick wooden doors.

She knew where she was going, so I followed. "This group is a little weird," she warned. "My shrink told me I have to go once a month. But the facilitator is great. And some of the women have really interesting stories."

"What do you mean a little weird?" I asked.

"You'll see," she said. "It's a general TG support group, so we get all kinds."

She wasn't kidding. There were about fifteen people in the room when we walked in. Natalie introduced me to the facilitator while I was still getting my bearings. She was a woman about my height with a halo of blond hair and bright eyes. She had the smallest nose and I felt a pang of jealousy. Natalie said she was some kind of psychologist, and I wondered how she ended up facilitating a group of transgender people. How did regular people get interested in us? Did she know someone or were we just research to her? Or could you actually make money with a psychology practice aimed at the transgender community? Maybe in the Cities it was possible.

"Elizabeth," she said, holding out her hand.

"This is Emily," Natalie said.

"Glad to have you, welcome."

We had a few more minutes before we started, so Natalie introduced me to more people with a dizzying array of descriptors. I met Renee, a woman in her mid-fifties who had begun her transitioning process recently and looked like someone's plain grandmother with the hands of a lumberjack. Vivianna was half-Asian, half-Spanish with the body of a ballet dancer. Natalie assured me twice that she'd been born male, though I found that hard to believe. Steve was an average-sized guy with short brown hair and a goatee.

"Shouldn't he shave?" I asked quietly, thinking about how I couldn't stand my own facial hair.

"He's FTM."

My brain took a second to translate: female-to-male. He'd been born with a girl's body. I took another look. It was impossible to tell.

There was another female-to-male member of the group, Mark, who looked like a teenager but dressed like he was older. Then there were a couple of people who very clearly looked like men in dresses. And one who looked like a man in a dress trying very hard not to look like a man in a dress but failing. "Those two are just cross-dressers," Natalie said. She indicated the third. "And she's just a little off-balance."

Elizabeth called the meeting to order and we all went around and said something about ourselves and what was going on in our lives. Renee had been at the same job for twenty years and still dressed as a man to go to work. She was trying to figure out how to talk to her HR department about coming to work as a woman. *That's going to be mind-bending for them*, I thought. Steve wanted a girlfriend but wasn't sure he'd find someone to accept him for who he was. Vivianna gave an update about her and her husband's quest to adopt a child.

When it came around to me, I tried to think of something intelligent to say. "I'm Emily," I said, feeling slightly ridiculous using that name with my deep voice and monstrously lanky body. "I'm in high school, and I'm trying to figure out how to talk to my parents. I have a good therapist and a really great girlfriend."

There was scattered applause and welcomes.

"That therapist will really help," Vivianna said. "I worked with one for almost a year and when I came out to my parents it was such a non-issue. I was in my early twenties and living on my own by then, but they said they'd always suspected and my mother said she always wanted a daughter. I have three brothers. I hope it's like that for you."

Steve spoke next. "Mine said they understood, but they keep screwing up my name and my pronoun."

"Oh that sucks so bad," Natalie told him. "It just feels so invalidating, doesn't it? You really look great, though, no one would read you."

To "read" someone was to see that they'd been born the other gender from the one they were presenting to the world. Natalie meant that no one would see Steve as anything other than a guy, and I thought she was right. How embarrassing to look like a guy to everyone and still have your parents call you "she."

"My parents threw me out," Mark said. "I was seventeen, and I ended up homeless for a couple of years. I'm working on forgiving them, but I'm not sure I ever want to see them again."

As the group was breaking up, Elizabeth sat next to me. "Was it helpful to come today?" she asked.

"It was okay," I said. "I think I have a lot of work to do."

She looked me in the eyes. "You won't regret it. If it's really what you want, you'll never look back."

"I know," I said. "It just seems so hard."

"Everyone has to go through a journey to become themselves. It's just more of a challenge for some than others, but a greater challenge also means a greater opportunity."

"Right," I said, unconvinced.

She opened her purse and pulled out her wallet, sliding out a small picture from behind the credit cards. "I don't show this to a lot of people," she said. "But I think you need to see it."

I looked down at the image of a young man glaring angrily at the camera, his hair hastily brushed to one side, and his brows lowered menacingly. He'd set his lips in a thin line, but that didn't disguise the full bow shape of his mouth that looked exactly like Elizabeth's. I looked up at her. The only similarities were the shape of her face, her lips and her nose. Anyone else would have assumed they'd been siblings.

"No," I said. There was no way that had been her. I felt like an idiot for assuming she wasn't one of us, and at the same time, I was thrilled.

"Twenty-seven years ago."

"Wow, you think I could look like you?"

"No, I think you could look like yourself. And I think you will look beautiful." She took the picture back and put it away. "You're welcome here anytime."

"Thanks," I told her, smiling.

On the way back to the car, Natalie asked, "Isn't she cool? She went to Europe in the eighties to get the surgery."

When I dropped Natalie off at her house, she paused and fished in her purse. "Hey, this isn't really kosher, and I wouldn't do this for anyone else, but with you stuck out there in the boonies and everything…" She handed me a small prescription bottle.

The label said Spironolactone and had her name on it. I turned it over in my hand. "How? You can't give me yours."

She smiled. "I told my doctor that I accidentally threw out my hormones when I was cleaning up. There are two kinds in there, the Spironolactone is an anti-androgen, it blocks testosterone production, and the round blue ones are Estrofem. You shouldn't start with that whole dose of that. Break them up and do a quarter of a pill for a few weeks and work up like that. That should last you a couple months and maybe by then we can figure out how to get you your own supply. I don't think my doctor will go for the 'lost it' thing more than once."

"Thank you so much."

"Take 'em with a meal," she said and flashed me a grin. "And for goodness sake, hide them well. It's easier to explain hard drugs to your parents than hormones."

I laughed and hugged her. "It's wonderful, thanks."

I drove back to Liberty trying to imagine what it would be like to be able to go through my days without always having to remember to be a guy. Elizabeth transitioned twenty-seven years ago and she was only in her middle age now. She'd already lived more than half her life as a woman. What if I could just be myself all the time?

When I got home, Mikey was watching TV with Dad. Mom was in the bedroom we kept as an office for paying bills and stuff. I went up to her and leaned on the filing cabinet. She was sitting at the desk sorting through a pile of mail with her hair messy as it usually was on weekends. She wouldn't wear sweatpants around the house, but she had on a pair of loose terrycloth pants and a sweater jacket.

"How was your trip to the city?" she asked distractedly.

"It was cool," I said. "I saw something unusual."

"Hmm, what?" she asked as she dropped an envelope into a short pile on the desk and picked up the next piece of mail.

"A woman who used to be a man."

"What?" she pivoted in her chair to face me. "How?"

"I guess surgery," I said, trying to sound super-super casual.

"How did you know?" she asked. Her eyes narrowed and her lips pressed together tightly at the end of the question.

"She told me. She said sometimes women get born into men's bodies—"

"You were talking to strange…people?"

"In the middle of the mall, it was harmless," I said. "I can take care of myself. I just thought it was interesting that that's possible."

"Chris," Mom said in her stern voice. "I don't want you going into the city alone, and you certainly don't need to spend time talking to freaks like that. If that happens again, you get up and leave."

"It was just a conversation, Mom, she wasn't hitting on me."

"You don't know what people like that are thinking. You're a good-looking young man and you need to be more careful. Promise me you'll watch out for yourself."

"Sure, Mom."

She stood up and gave me a kiss on the cheek. "Don't tell that to your dad, he would flip."

"Okay," I said. "I guess I'll go work on my homework."

I went upstairs and lay down on my bed. I felt torn in half. One half was happy and excited about life. She'd gone to a support group meeting and got hormones and she had a girlfriend who loved her. The other half was a papier-mâché shell that looked like a guy on the outside and was hollow within. His emptiness was full of echoes of my mother's voice saying "freaks like that," "you're a good-looking young man," and "your dad would flip."

I fell asleep staring at nothing and dreamed that the papier-mâché man was choking me to death.

CHAPTER FOURTEEN

I started taking the anti-androgen and the first fraction of an estrogen pill with breakfast the next morning. I didn't expect to feel different right away, but I did feel lighter when I went to school. That was probably the placebo effect, or just pure hopefulness. Yes, my mom thought transsexual people were freaks—that wasn't really unusual for a woman who'd spent all her life in rural Minnesota. She'd come around when she saw how happy I was...right?

During science class, I imagined the estrogen soaking into all the cells of my body, reassuring each little bit of me that everything was going to be all right. I sailed through the day. In psych class I gave Mr. Cooper the decoy paper that Claire had emailed me the day before. I'd changed a few details, but her story was very good at imagining what it was like to be a boy waking up as a girl. A lot better than my version.

The week waltzed by and on Thursday I met Claire after school to go to Dr. Mendel with me. I'd told Mom she didn't need to come along just to make sure that I was going and that I planned to bring Claire so we could talk about "boy-girl" stuff. That did the trick.

Claire and I sat on the couch in Dr. Mendel's office. Claire's fingers tapped out a pattern on the arm and she kept crossing her legs one way and then the other as Dr. Mendel closed the door and settled into the chair across from us. I thought Claire might have worn extra black for the visit because she had on black cobweb earrings and black bracelets in addition to the usual black shirt, jeans and boots. I'd made it all the way down to sweater number six this week, and Dr. Mendel was in a cream colored jacket over a plum shell and gray pants.

"Thank you for coming," Dr. Mendel said to Claire. "I've heard a lot of wonderful things about you. And you also game together?"

"I play a paladin mostly," Claire said. She thought that Dr. Mendel asking me what kinds of characters I played was supercool, so I was glad Dr. Mendel started there again.

"It's no wonder that you're Emily's protector in the real world then."

"You think so?" Claire asked. "I mean, that I'm a protector?"

"Yeah," I said without waiting for Dr. Mendel to answer. "I'd be in a lot worse shape without you around."

"But I kind of freaked out there at the start," Claire said.

"That's natural. Emily had years to figure this out. You had to adapt to a lot of new knowledge in just a few days," Dr. Mendel told her.

"When you put it that way, I guess I am pretty awesome," Claire responded with a grin. "So, what do we do here?"

"I was hoping I could help answer any questions you have so that Emily doesn't have to field all of them, and then if we have time I'd like to hear more about Emily's early experiences of herself, and I bet you would too."

Claire looked at me and then back at the doctor. "Totally," she said. She uncrossed her legs and put her hands on her knees. "Questions, hmm. I read a ton of stuff and it's still jumbled up in my head, so I'm sorry if I don't say things the right way."

"It's okay," I told her and squeezed her shoulder lightly. I wanted to know what questions she still had and Dr. Mendel was right that I felt grateful not to be the only one to answer all of them.

"What's the difference between transgender and transsexual and gender nonconforming?" Claire asked. "Lots of cultures seem to have had men who dressed like women, for example, ancient Sumer, Greece and Rome, some Native American cultures. And it sounds like some people are okay just dressing as women or living as women but not having all those surgeries. How do you know what's what?"

"I don't want to just cross-dress," I said.

Dr. Mendel held up her hand before I could go on. "Emily, let Claire have her questions. It's a good question. There's a difference between gender nonconformity and gender dysphoria. Many people feel that their gender expression doesn't fit the cultural norm for their gender and when that's the case, most of the time, they may choose to identify as transgender, which is a broader category than transsexual."

She went on, "I think everyone has had some experience of gender nonconformity. When I went to college in the '60s there were quite a few people who felt that women wearing pants was still gender nonconforming. I'm glad we got rid of that idea. And when my husband took a few years off teaching to raise our children and research a book, he really had to struggle with cultural opinions about a man staying at home with the children."

"My mom thinks my goth look is gender nonconforming because I don't wear bright colors and show off my boobs and paint my face," Claire offered.

"Precisely," Dr. Mendel said. "Now, gender dysphoria specifically refers to the distress a person feels when their gender identity doesn't match the sex they were assigned at birth. And even gender dysphoria isn't an unchanging condition. There are children who experience gender dysphoria but for whom it doesn't persist. Not every feminine boy or masculine girl is necessarily transsexual."

"Aw, I was just about to go around diagnosing my other friends," Claire said with a grin.

Dr. Mendel smiled back at her with genuine humor. "I did a lot of diagnosis from the sidelines when I was in school. I do want both of you to know that if gender dysphoria is present in childhood and persists into adolescence, there's a very high chance that it will remain into adulthood unless treated."

"Mom shouldn't wait for me to grow out of it then," I offered.

"Neither should you," Dr. Mendel said.

I thought about that. "You're right, there's still a part of me that keeps thinking if I do the boy thing enough it will stick."

"There are plenty of transsexual women who've joined the military or taken up extremely masculine professions to see if they could get maleness to stick to them and not have to come out as women born into male bodies," Dr. Mendel said.

"I don't want to do that," I told her. I felt a chill shudder down my back just under the skin. In junior high for over a year I was really convinced that I wanted to go into auto mechanics when I grew up. What a disaster that would have been.

"Why don't you talk about what you do want," Dr. Mendel prompted.

The rest of the hour was great. I told Claire more of the stories from when I was little, like dressing up in Mom's clothes and playing with the girl who lived down the street as if we were two girls.

***

Maybe it was all the talking and support that made me feel bold that weekend. I didn't plan ahead, I just got in my car on Saturday and started driving in the opposite direction from the Cities until I ended up in Annandale. I pulled over in a residential area in front of a house that looked dark, and got the duffel out of the back. It now had Claire's makeup kit in it as well. It took me over half an hour to change in the car and do my makeup in the rearview mirror. I didn't know what else to do. I couldn't very well go into either gender of bathroom as a man and come out as a woman.

The other problem was that I really didn't have any good shoes. I had some black boots that were more punk than anything, so I'd thrown those in the car with me and they'd have to do with the long skirt. They looked vaguely stylish. Also I only had a hat for my head. The good news was that my hair had grown long enough in the back to hang down past my collar in a few thick curls. The bad news was that it still looked too short for my taste, but I couldn't do anything about that now.

I tried to get a good look at myself in the mirror, but it's hard to see how you look from a two-inch-by-six-inch reflection. If I turned to the right, I looked pretty girlish, but from other angles, not so good. If I kept my eyes down, I should do pretty well. I'd shaved my face to within an inch of my life that morning and the foundation was thick enough to cover any lingering trouble there. Plus I felt like the estrogen was softening my skin already, though it was probably way too soon.

I figured I'd try a really quick trip into a store and see how I did. I went to Walmart. There were enough people there that I could blend in, and I thought I should get a purse before I went anywhere else.

I walked in and across the store without actually taking a full breath. My shoes sounded loud on the floor. Out of my peripheral vision, I thought I saw a woman turn and look at me, but I didn't stop to find out. My heart was beating against my breastbone like a person pounding on a door.

In an empty aisle of purses I had to stop and make myself fill my lungs a few times so I wouldn't just pass out. The store smelled like lemon cleaner and the dark musk of leather. I smelled like iron-edged fear.

I tried to make myself look at the individual purses, but my hand shook when I took one off the long metal rack. I put that one back, it reminded me of my mother's, and grabbed a small, plain black purse on my way to the cash registers. Then I paused. I was supposed to buy control top pantyhose. Someone online said that was the key to "tucking" successfully. I had no idea what size or where to look, but the store had only a couple dozen people in it and so far no alarms had gone off and no one was staring at me as far as I could tell.

I followed the signs to lingerie and found myself staring at a long, long aisle of pantyhose. Tiered row after row of white, gray and tan packages with colorful labels stretched into the distance. This would be a good time to ask for help, I thought, except that I hadn't worked on my voice enough. I couldn't actually say anything without giving myself away.

Good Lord, I was an idiot. I took a deep breath and then another.

I walked down the row until I saw "control top" and then tried to read the sizing chart on the back. I had a few options, so I took one of each and made for the registers.

I picked the one with a young, dark-skinned girl with a head-scarf. She looked like she'd come over from a foreign country recently, and I was hoping I'd seem like just another American oddity to her. "Good morning," she said in heavily accented English and rang up the items. "That'll be twenty-eight fifty-three, miss."

My heart soared. I unfolded two crumpled twenties from my palm and handed them to her. The change went into my new purse, the stockings into a bag, and I stepped out into the fresh, cold air.

"Miss" reverberated in my head all the way back to the car. I'd done it! For the first time I was out in public as a woman and at least for a few minutes, I passed. The elation mixed with the caffeine from the bottled depth charge cold coffee drink I'd sipped all the way out here and it seemed like my heavy boots floated inches above the ground. I felt goofy about being so excited, but after years of having "boy" and "son" land like shrapnel in me, being called "miss" felt amazing.

I downed the rest of the coffee and drove the next two miles to the little mall in Annandale. Now that I was out in public, I didn't want to have to change back into my boy clothes and go home.

Okay, I told myself in the mall parking lot, *this has got to be a quick exercise; I'm going to walk through and out because I can't actually talk to anyone.* I was going to have to practice with my voice a lot more in the near future. Maybe I should take voice lessons. I wondered if Mom would go for that.

It wasn't noon yet and the mall's main corridors looked almost empty. Two women with babies in strollers walked along one side of the main corridor, and I picked the other side so I could avoid them. An old woman holding onto the arm of an old man passed me but didn't look up at my face. I went from one end to the other and then started to stroll back. I really needed new shoes. Through the windows I looked at a few pairs. They had a DSW, which was a discount shoe warehouse that skimped on staff to keep their prices low so you had to pick out your own shoes and try them on without assistance. I should be able to try on something in there without having to fend off a salesperson in pantomime.

Quickly I found the section of women's boots, but I didn't know much about women's shoes and had no idea what size I was. I should have brought Claire with me. I put two different shoes next to my foot and guessed that I was a size eleven or twelve in women's sizes, but I wasn't nearly comfortable enough to take off my boots and try one on. What if someone came up to me? Would I end up running out of the mall with my boots in my hands?

With a sigh, I gave up and headed back in the direction of the car. Claire wasn't terribly fond of shopping, but if I threw in a movie, she'd probably come with me. Three junior high school kids walking in front of their parents stared at me as I passed and my heart started thrumming hard against my breastbone. Did they know? I turned away from them and kept walking. I should have waited until I could do a better job at this. Thank goodness no one here knew me.

Unfortunately, my racing heart along with the huge bottled coffee meant that I had to pee so badly that it hurt. All the people in the mall were down at the other end where the better shops were. This end just held the administrative office and the restrooms.

I paused in the hall to the restrooms and waited for a few long minutes to see if there was anyone in the women's restroom. No one came out. I really wanted to see what I looked like in something larger than a rearview mirror, and I was literally hopping from one foot to the other. If I went out to the car, I'd have to wait until after I changed and then go find a restroom at a crappy gas station.

I ducked into the women's restroom and looked at myself in the mirror. The hat looked cute and so did my makeup, but my eyebrows were terrible and the whole size and ratio of my body still looked wrong. A passerby might think I was a girl, and then again might not. It all depended on what their sense of reality included; I either looked like a very boyish girl, or a boy very much in drag.

The outfit was good because it avoided the loud and dramatic, but I really needed to work on my ability to walk and to speak. For the first time out, though, it was a huge victory.

I turned toward the stalls. There were so many of them and no urinals. This was for sure the first time in my life that a restroom actually made me happy.

You don't have time, I told myself sternly. *What are you going to do if someone comes in? Go.*

I quickly stepped into a stall and sat down to pee. It was so clean in here. Not just the floor but the walls of the stall were almost bare. I'd never been to this mall before, but in Liberty's two tiny malls both of the men's bathrooms were covered with disgusting graffiti. I didn't have anything against graffiti, it was the subject matter that disgusted me. The scrawls tended universally toward anti-gay sentiments, woman bashing and bragging about sexual prowess. In this stall there was a sticker about breast cancer awareness posted on one side and on the other in looping handwriting the message, "You are really beautiful."

The restroom door opened and closed and then a heavy fist pounded on the stall door. I leaped off the toilet and pulled up my underpants so fast I nearly tore them and the skirt right off.

"All right, sir, come out of there," a man demanded.

When I got the door open, a potato-shaped security guard was glaring at me.

"Come with me," he said.

I did. We ended up in the mall security office, which was a large closet off that same short hallway, furnished with a desk, one chair behind it and two in front of it. I got one of the chairs in front of it.

"All right, son," the man said. "What do you think you're doing?"

"I'm sorry," I said, while frantically running through stories in my mind. My voice sounded awful because it was not only too low but also rough with fear.

"You're damn right you are. Jesus Christ, look at you. What's your name?"

"Jim," I said. "Jim Harding."

"You better not be lying to me. Let's see some ID."

"I didn't bring any," I said, honestly. I opened the purse and showed him it was empty except for the money.

"Where you from?"

"The Cities," I said.

"They tolerate this kind of shit there?" he asked, then sat back in the chair. "What do you think you're doing in a ladies' restroom? You're some kind of pervert, aren't you? You think you're going to see something in there? You looking at girls or just like to pretend you are one?"

I felt so far outside myself I might have been in the next

county. This had gone beyond nightmarish into the bizarre and unbelievable. I knew my heart was beating unbearably fast, but I couldn't actually feel it anymore. My body was cold and numb.

"No," I said with some emphasis.

"I suppose you're some kind of fag," he suggested.

"No," I said, equally vehemently.

"Well then what, exactly, are you doing trolling around in women's clothing, boy?"

For a moment, I considered telling him some version of the truth, which might feel like less of a betrayal of myself than lying outright. I could tell him that I was transsexual and that my doctor said I needed to spend a certain amount of time living as a woman. I was certain he had no idea there were internationally accepted guidelines that health professionals used to support the wellbeing of people with gender identity disorders.

As good as it would feel to be honest, I worried that he could try to hold me here and make me call my parents. I certainly didn't want him saying anything about transsexualism to them.

My neck shook with the effort not to put my head in my hands. If my parents had to come here and see me in a skirt…I was doomed. They'd never let me out of the house again, or they'd never let me into the house again, and Dad would certainly stop talking to me. I had to find another way out of this situation, even if I had to lie through my teeth to do it.

"I lost a bet," I said. "I'm on the swim team, see." I flexed my shoulders for verisimilitude, a gesture that I'm sure looked monstrous in that outfit. "And we had a race and the loser, who clearly was me, had to dress up like a girl, with makeup and everything, and go to a mall and buy something. So I tried to pick a mall where none of the guys would see me."

"But the restroom?" he asked.

I shrugged. "I drank a lot of coffee. I couldn't go into the guys' like this, and it's freezing outside."

He shook his head in disgust. "If I ever see you in this mall again, I am hauling you to the police station, understand? And, if you want my advice, don't lose any more bets. Get out."

I did. I ran for my car and drove out of that messed-up town. At a rest stop I pulled over and, when I'd stopped shaking enough to use my fingers, awkwardly changed clothes in the car. I wiped off all the makeup and got out of the car to throw the used wipes away at an outdoor trash can, not bothering with my jacket. The cold made me feel real.

I stood out there for a long time thinking about how incredibly stupid I was and wondering what the hell made me think I would ever make it in the world as a woman. The whole scene with the guard had been miserable, but the worst part was lying, making up that whole ridiculous story about losing a bet, having to pretend I was a guy all over again. How could I make my way in the world if I couldn't stand up for myself?

I looked at the big green trash can in front of me, wondering if I should just throw away my girl clothes and give up. Except that everyone did that at least once, and then they showed up years later in places like GenderPeace and Natalie's support group saying they wished they'd never done that. I wanted to learn from someone's mistakes, even if I wasn't so good at learning from my own.

And for just that second when I'd considered coming out to that guy, telling him I was transsexual, under all the fear and dread, it felt good. Deep down under the pounding heart and the sweat breaking out on my skin, under my burning eyes and clenched throat, I knew who I was. Did I have the courage to be that person?

It was part of the World Professional Association for Transgender Health's standards of care that transsexual people had to spend a good chunk of time, months or a year, living as the gender they were transitioning to before surgery of any kind was performed, and I could have recited all that to him, chapter and verse. I could have stood up for myself. But I couldn't risk telling him the truth.

I turned back to the car and slammed myself into it. What was the use of knowing all this information that I couldn't use?

When I got back to the house I was still shivering, which turned out to be the start of a fever.

***

I missed school on Monday and Tuesday, miserably situated in front of droning daytime television with a head full of snot. It almost kept me distracted from reflecting on Saturday's horror, but every few hours it would unfold in front of me again and play itself out. I'd be left second-guessing myself over and over. I shouldn't have used the bathroom. I should have told him the truth. I should be on real hormones, not some I got from a friend. I should tell my parents. I should shoot myself. I should drink more hot tea and stop acting like a morose idiot.

Claire called and checked on me every day, but I didn't tell her what had happened. It was too stupid to bear repeating. She knew something was wrong, though.

On Thursday, she came with me to Dr. Mendel, but I asked if she'd wait in the waiting area this time. She agreed and opened the book she'd brought for just such an occasion.

I told Dr. Mendel what had happened, and she actually had tears in her eyes at the end of the story.

"I'm sorry," she said. "You should never have been treated that way."

"I was stupid," I said.

"Just impatient," she said. "What actions are you taking for yourself?"

"I'm working on my voice," I said. "Sometimes after school when I have some time alone in my car. And…a friend gave me some estrogen I'm taking and an anti-androgen. I know it's illegal, but it's only a little bit."

Her eyebrows went up. "I understand that you want to be on hormones very badly, but there are medical risks. Taking hormones can put stress on your heart, liver and other systems in your body. I'd like to see you visiting a doctor who is knowledgeable about hormone use for transition so you can get regular checkups. I know two doctors in the Cities that I can recommend, but you'll need your parents' permission."

"They're going to freak out," I said. "I've been hinting to Mom and it's not going well."

I told her what had happened the two times I'd tried to bring something up. She started laughing out loud at the impotence story and I laughed along with her, feeling each burst of air loosen my chest a little.

"Sometimes it takes a while for parents to adjust," she said. "We can come up with a plan together. You have to be prepared for them to be upset at first and not assume that's the end of the world."

"Okay," I agreed, though I was fairly certain it would be the end of the world.

"Before we get to that, I want to spend the rest of this visit and our next few sessions really talking about the risks and benefits of the transition process. I can write you a letter for the physician who would prescribe hormones, but I want us to talk through all of this together first. There are people with gender dysphoria who choose only hormones and not surgery and even some who opt for neither."

"I know, I know," I said. "I've been looking at all of this for years. I know there are risks to the surgery and some people decide they don't want it, but that's years down the road. I can't even afford it yet and anyway, I'd get the facial surgery first."

I paused and took a deep breath because she was just looking at me with that open, clear sky look that made me feel like no matter what I said it was okay.

"I'm sorry, I feel like everyone wants to challenge me on this," I said.

"That's not what we're here for. We're going to create the life you want for yourself. I'm just asking that we start at the beginning and go through all the steps."

"I can do that," I told her. "Where do we start?"

"I have some basic psychological tests I'd like to give you. I see that Dr. Webber tested you for depression but I'd like to get my own results. It's common with transsexualism to struggle with depression and anxiety, and I want to get a good feel for how much of that you're dealing with."

I cracked a big grin. "You mean I shouldn't lie on the tests this time?"

She laughed. "That is precisely what I mean. And I want you to understand that if you come out of this office with a diagnosis of gender identity disorder, that does not mean that you as a person are disordered or diseased or that there's something wrong with who you are."

"Thank you," I told her.

We decided to start the tests on the next visit so that I'd have plenty of time for them and ended the hour just chatting. As Dr. Mendel walked me to the door, she said, "Take care of yourself. And if you want to go shopping dressed as a girl, get support, don't do it alone."

In the waiting room, Claire stood up as I came out of the office. "Is Chris okay?" she asked Dr. Mendel through the open door.

"Yes," Dr. Mendel said. "Absolutely fine, but in need of some cheering up, and maybe a shopping trip in the near future." She left us after that and Claire looked at me questioningly.

"Shopping?" she asked.

"I want to go shopping as a girl," I said quietly, after making sure there was no one near.

Claire sat back down in the chair she'd been waiting in. I worried that I'd frayed her patience past the breaking point and, when she pulled out her phone, thought she might actually be calling her mother to come get her.

"What's Natalie's number?" she asked.

It took a moment for the question to register, and then I told her, following it with, "Wait, why are you calling her?"

But it was too late. She'd dialed and had the phone to her ear. "Natalie? Hey, it's Claire, you know, from the boonies. Yeah. Yeah. Right here. Yeah, but we need a favor. She wants to go shopping. Sure. Yeah, it's my cell. Cool."

She hung up and stood up. "All right, she's calling me back."

"That's it?" I asked.

She shrugged. "No, I reserve the right to freak out about this later when you're not looking."

I looped my arm over her shoulders. "You are so cool. Do you know that's the first time you've called me 'she'?"

"Don't rub it in. Come on She-Ra Princess of Power, take me home."

"Does that make you He-Man?"

She laughed. "I guess so. Gender nonconformity, here I come!"

***

The next morning on my way to study hall, she handed me a note. It said: "Overnight in the city. Set it up with your folks. Have them call Nat's mom tonight. She'll handle the 'boy thing.'"

What boy thing? I thought, but that was answered as soon as I got home and broached the subject with my mom.

"You can't have a sleepover with two girls in the city—one of whom we don't even know!" she said.

"Oh, yeah, you're supposed to call her mother." I handed Mom a sheet of paper with Natalie's home number on it.

"How do you even know this girl?" Mom asked.

"We met online. She plays the same games that Claire and I do. We've hung out with her a few times. Her mom's a successful lawyer." The part about games wasn't true, but that last bit was the important part. It was meant to convey a sense of safety to my mother and a sense that I was spending time with the right kind of people.

Mom sighed and went to the phone. The conversation went: "Hello? Yes. Yes, Chris's mom. Good to meet you too, Susan. Online games, he said. Well, I wonder that too." Pause and a laugh. "Really? Oh separate rooms, of course. A daughter in college, that's nice. Princeton? My goodness. And you'll be there all night with them?" Pause and laugh again. "Oh no, no that's not necessary. Yes, that would be nice. Yes, thank you. Goodbye."

She hung up and turned to me. "Well, I suppose it's all right. They sound like very nice people. She said you'll have your own room for the night. She even offered to drive out here so we could meet her. Isn't that nice?"

"Yeah," I said, thinking that Natalie's mom had to be fantastic to make that offer.

"Go have a good time," she said. "And tell me all about it. I bet they have a wonderful house."

I smiled. "Okay, Mom."

***

I picked up Claire at four on Saturday and we drove into the city. Her mom had also talked with Natalie's mom and experienced a similarly reassuring conversation. I wondered what it was they thought we would do without parental supervision? Maybe an all-night drunken, pot-smoking orgy. Of course if Mom knew what we were really up to, she might have preferred the orgy.

Natalie's family lived in the northern part of the western suburbs in a sprawling two-story house. When we pulled up, Natalie came out in tan boots that had white, furry cuffs on them, and a coat also with a line of white fur around the hood, to help lug our overnight bags in, along with the secret duffel.

"My brother's at a friend's until tomorrow afternoon," she said when we all crammed into the entryway. "And Dad has locked himself in the master bedroom. He tries to be cool, but this girl stuff creeps him out sometimes. So we have the house to ourselves." She turned and yelled into the house, "Mom, they're here!"

I expected Natalie's mom to be kind of glamorous, but she wasn't. She had dark hair shot through with gray that she'd looped into a bun at the base of her neck. She had the same big, dark eyes that Natalie had, but a smaller chin and nose.

"Welcome," she said. "You can call me Susan, I much prefer that to 'Natalie's mom' or, heaven forebid, 'ma'am.' Come on in. We have enough beds for you if you want, but I thought you girls might like the lower level for a full slumber party atmosphere."

She went toward the downstairs and Claire followed, but I didn't know what to do. She'd said "girls," did that include me? At the top of the stairs she paused and looked back at me, beckoning. I guess I *was* one of the girls. Grinning, I followed.

The lower level had been set up as an entertainment center, with a big TV and a huge L-shaped couch. Three sleeping bags were rolled up at the end of the couch and a small stack of blankets lay next to them.

"Make yourselves comfortable, I'll go put the pizza in the oven," she said and headed back up the stairs.

I followed her.

"You told my mom I was going to be in a separate room," I said.

"Yes," Natalie's mom…Susan said. "If you're more comfortable, you can have Natalie's sister's room, but if you want to sleep in the lower level, you could just roll a sleeping bag out on the left side of the TV, which is, technically, a separate room, or at least would be if we hadn't torn down that wall. I think it's still listed as separate on the property report."

I smiled. "You planned that."

"Natalie did," she said. "She said it would be good for you to have a girls' night and promised me no funny business."

"No ma'am," I said, unable to stop grinning. "Why are you so cool about all this? I think my mom would totally freak out."

She opened the freezer and took out two pizzas. "I did some freaking out," she said. "But, I don't know if you'll understand this until you're a mother, there are much worse things in life than gender identity disorder. There were nights I'd lie awake and wonder if Nat was going to kill herself and why it was happening and if I'd be able to stop her. I'd try to think of how she might do it, and to take away anything I thought she could use to hurt herself, but it was never enough for me to know she'd be safe. I had some rough nights after she told me what the problem was, why she was so depressed, but I knew…after that I knew she'd live, that she'd grow up and actually have a good life. That's a gift. That's what a parent really wants for their kids. I think your mother will come to understand that too. She does love you and she wants you to be happy."

"She's not as…educated as you," I ventured.

She laughed. "Law school doesn't prepare you for this, believe me. Your mom can learn the same things I did. Now come on, Claire said you need shopping therapy tomorrow, and we have another little surprise."

The surprise turned out to be a couple of the wigs Natalie used to wear before her hair grew out and that her parents hadn't gotten around to giving away yet. The fit was tight, but with the right bobby pins, the plain brown, wavy hair would work. I think I spent an hour in the bathroom staring at myself with the hair falling past my shoulders. Without makeup, I looked kind of silly, but I could start to see how it would come together.

I counted my lucky stars that I'd been born at a good time. In earlier decades, earlier centuries, people like me had had to content themselves with just dressing as women, but I could actually have my body altered to match my sense of myself. I lifted the hair off my forehead and looked at the ridge under my eyebrows. I was definitely going to need to save up a lot of money this summer, and the next and probably for a few after that, but I would figure out how to get the facial surgery that would take away the caveman aspects. Natalie hadn't needed it and I envied her.

Claire banged on the door. "You going to stay in there all night?" When I came out she added, "You are such a girl."

I'm not sure she meant it as a compliment, but I took it as one anyway. Then we all sat around, including Nat's mom, and painted our toenails. We talked fairly unsuccessfully about makeup and movie stars for a few minutes, but I had a lack of knowledge and Claire protested the whole thing, so we ended up talking about school and politics and what the world had been like when Natalie's mom was a kid. Okay, during that last part we just listened politely.

Natalie's mom showed me where to put a sleeping bag so that I was technically in another room, and Natalie scared up a pair of silk pajama bottoms that fit me rather than the boxer shorts that were all I'd had. I lay awake for a long time feeling my heart floating in my chest.

CHAPTER FIFTEEN

CLAIRE

She lay awake for a long time too, dealing with a much stickier situation. *If my boyfriend is a girl*, she wondered, *what does that make me?*

Sure she could just say "a lesbian" and leave it at that, but that didn't answer the doubts gnawing at her. From what she'd seen and read, even a lot of lesbians weren't too keen about girls who dated girls who used to be boys. If she continued through all this with Chris, would she wake up one morning to find there was nowhere in the world where she belonged?

She almost laughed at that thought. When had she ever

been worried about belonging? But she'd never felt this kind of isolation before. When she provoked her mom and other kids at school with her goth look, or by saying she was bisexual, or by entertaining the possibility of being a lesbian, or by spouting esoteric bits of poetry or religion, that was she herself drawing the boundary and saying what groups she was and wasn't in. Suddenly, a whole lot of lines had been drawn *for* her.

As she often did when something bothered her, she tried to pull apart the different aspects of it. Number one was that she could end up even more of an outsider. Number two, much as she hated to admit it, was that Chris was getting more attention than she was. He'd been the quiet guy for most of their relationship, and now, at least here, all the attention was on him. Claire didn't begrudge him that, he certainly deserved some care. She just wanted more of the spotlight.

Number three was an uglier aspect than the first two. She accepted that Chris didn't have a choice about this situation, that he…or she, rather, had been born this way and had to go through all kinds of hell to get to a life that worked. But she had a choice about loving Chris. She could walk away, she could explore whether that fairly normal-looking kid in her history class really was interested in her.

She stared at Chris in his sleeping bag across the room. Who loved someone like that? Was she that desperate to be weird? Was there some way in which all of this was still about her?

No, she decided. She didn't want to walk away. She'd come to know Chris and this whole business about sex and gender didn't change the person she'd gotten to know. Well, except for making her a girl. But in some way she'd always been a girl, just in a really good disguise.

Claire stared up at the ceiling. It was a gray waffle board pattern, and she missed the plain white of her bedroom. Why was she here? Had she really needed to come along on this mission? She could have just sent Chris to spend the weekend with Natalie and stayed home.

Sometimes when she prayed or talked to God she had the

feeling of a huge intelligence looking at her, usually smiling. It was there now, surrounding her. *Trust me*, it seemed to say.

She rolled up onto her hands and knees and crawled across the basement floor to where Chris was lying on top of his sleeping bag with a light blanket over his legs. His eyes were still open. Claire rolled down against Chris's side and he put his arm around her. She took a deep breath and stopped—he smelled different. Chris had always smelled like salt and sand and warm metal, but now the metallic part was fading. Claire knew she was smelling the lotion he'd put on earlier in addition to the natural smell, but still there had been a change. An edginess was gone and she kind of missed it.

But this was good too. Would his smell keep changing? But that wasn't really the most important question. *When are you going to stop thinking of Chris as him?* she asked herself. *You know she doesn't like that.*

Oh shut up, she told the highly evolved part of her brain, *I want to hold onto something of him.*

But why? She draped her arm over Chris's stomach. This was all she needed to hold onto, she thought. Just the person.

CHAPTER SIXTEEN

In the morning, Natalie's mom made us eggs and bacon. Her dad came down for a few minutes to eat with us. He looked at me for a while but didn't say anything. Then he excused himself to go to the gym.

"What's up with your dad?" Claire asked when Natalie's mom was out of the room.

"He's really my stepdad," she said. "But he and Mom have been married for, like, twelve years, so I figure he gets to be a dad too. He's actually pretty sweet about the whole thing, but I think it scares him. I think he's afraid that someone's going to show up in the middle of the night and take his guy parts away and turn him into a girl."

Claire laughed, but I wondered how often people respond badly to transgendered people because somewhere inside them they're afraid it's going to happen to them. "How about you?" I asked Claire teasingly. "Are you afraid the bad fairy is going to turn you into a boy?"

She cocked her head to one side, the way she did when she was thinking hard. "Kind of," she said. "I was thinking about that when I did your homework last week." She paused and poked my arm for emphasis. "If I just woke up as a guy, it might be kind of cool, but if I had all the memories of being in this body, and all the girl experiences I've had, and the dreams for my life, then yeah, I'd be totally freaked 'cause I'd know that wasn't really me, you know?"

"Boy do we," Natalie said.

Claire's mouth hung open. "Oh yeah," she managed. "I guess that is how it is for you. Everything inside you says one thing, but no one believes you. Wow, I never thought about it that clearly. It is just like how I'd feel if I were hit with the 'boy gun.'"

Natalie's mom came back in and Natalie started clearing the dishes. "Okay," she said. "Here's the plan. We have two showers, so Nat and Emily you're first. Then, Nat, you're doing Emily's makeup. Claire and I will sit in the living room and talk about politics." She grinned so we knew she was joking, though I suspected that was how it would go. "Then we are going to Southdale Mall to get Emily a decent pair of shoes and whatever else strikes our fancy. Natalie says you're not great with your voice, so I think you can just fake laryngitis. Anything you want to say, just whisper to one of us. We'll provide the cover story. Sound good?"

I nodded, thinking that heaven was probably populated with people like this.

Natalie gave me the upstairs shower and took the one in the basement, a generous gesture that I understood when I got into that shower. It had all sorts of fancy shampoos and soaps and scrubs. Except for the lure of shopping, I could have spent an hour in there.

Natalie knocked on the door as I was drying off. When I cracked it open, she pushed in and looked at me. "Nice legs," she said.

I kept the towel around my waist and tried not to blush.

"Here," she said, and set down two fist-sized packets of an indeterminate nature. "Use these in your bra."

"What are they?"

"Birdseed mostly, they're the best because they're pretty close to the feel and shape of real breasts. You can keep 'em."

"Thanks!"

She slipped out and I dressed quickly in case she was going to barge in again. I wanted to wear the brown pants, so I used the control-top hose that I'd cut off mid-thigh to tuck up between my legs and brace the parts that didn't really fit in girls' pants. Then I put on my bra and fit the falsies into the cups. Natalie had a point, they filled out the bra so much better than cotton balls. I pulled on my sweater and looked at myself in the mirror.

I looked weird. My body actually looked like an athletic girl's body, but with no waist. My face looked half-boy and half-girl. "Jeez, I'm an alien," I said, and pushed out the door in search of Natalie and makeup.

Half an hour later I was back in the bathroom and I looked a lot better this time. Natalie's mom had pinned the wig on in a way that gave me short bangs and long brown hair. I wasn't sure I'd wear my hair like that if I had a choice, but I was not going to argue right now. The wispy bangs covered my typically male sloping brow and the ridge over my eyes. Natalie's makeup job partly hid the other masculine planes of my face. I didn't exactly look pretty, but I could pass if I didn't talk.

When we got close to the mall, I started to feel extremely nervous, almost panicky. All I could think about was the stupid attempt I'd made by myself and that jackass security guard. I reached over and took Claire's hand and she squeezed my fingers.

"You look good," she said.

I couldn't tell how much of that was true and how much she was just trying to make me feel better, but I was pretty sure that no one we would run into at the mall would want to go toe-to-toe with Natalie's mom. She wore jeans but she'd put on a silk T-shirt and a navy blazer, along with thick gold hoop earrings, and I could see a hint of how tough and capable she must look in court. She parked a few hundred feet from the doors because the lot was almost full, and we had to carefully avoid the frozen-over slush puddles that were the land mines of a Minnesota spring. With a light dusting of snow on the ground, you'd think you were going to step on solid land until your foot broke through the paper-thin sheet of ice and a couple inches of freezing water soaked your shoe.

Inside the mall, it was hot so we took off our scarves and jackets right away. I carried mine under my right arm with my purse looped over my left shoulder. Natalie said the purse looked good for a thirty-second Walmart purchase. I hoped that was a compliment.

"I can't believe you tried this alone," she said. "I wouldn't have had the guts."

"I figured if I screwed it up, no one would know," I said quietly, and indeed they didn't know the horrible details.

Natalie's mom beelined for a shoe store. "What's your size?" she asked.

I shrugged, "Eleven maybe?"

Three minutes later I was sitting on the shoe bench with four pairs of boots around me, a salesman running to the back room for more, and Natalie and Claire arguing over styles. Boot in hand, I stopped to take a deep breath of shoe leather and polish. If I kept a photo album of life's central moments, I'd put this in. I wanted to be able to remember everything: the crazy fluorescent lights shining harshly on the red highlights of Natalie's hair, the way Claire bit her lip when she was listening to something she disagreed with, Natalie's mom calling all three of us "the girls," the way the salesman called me "miss" without even thinking about it.

Everything around me seemed so real, as if it had more weight and density than my former everyday life. I must have spent a lot of time not really looking at things until now. That made sense because I spent so much of it looking at myself and making sure I wasn't going to screw up.

I dropped right into the bit about laryngitis and figured out how to laugh soundlessly so I could join in the jokes Claire was making about women's shoe styles.

"Not the pointed toe," she said about one pair, and I leaned in to whisper to her, "Too witchy?" She cracked up and repeated it to Natalie and her mom.

The sales guy caught it and grinned. "Sorry about your voice," he said as he dropped off another load of boxes.

I smiled and shrugged.

"Does it hurt?" he asked.

I held up my thumb and forefinger with a small gap between them to signify "a little."

He laughed. "Girls, nothing keeps you from shopping, does it?"

I shook my head, but I couldn't stop grinning.

I felt like my heart had expanded to fill the whole store. It might sound silly, but I'd been crushed inside myself for so long that now that the binding was off, I wasn't sure if I wouldn't just keep on expanding until I encompassed everything.

"Earth to Emily," Claire said. "Bring the Moon landing home."

"Sorry," I mouthed.

She patted my shoulder, "Don't worry about it, you look like a kid at Christmas. I think you should get the brown pair. They'll go with the pants you love."

I did, along with a pair of black flats that Natalie recommended: my first girl shoes. I wore the brown pair out of the store, putting my guy boots in the bag.

We strolled down the mall, looking in windows and talking about who needed what. Natalie was interested in a new scarf, but she didn't really need one, and her mother was giving her the "you're over your limit" look. Claire suggested we hunt for a sweater sale. The end of winter was always a good time to pick up half-price finds.

After we looked in a few stores, Natalie's mom proposed lunch and we all filed into P.F. Chang's for tea and shared appetizers.

"Where are you girls from?" the waiter asked. He was a thick guy, probably a wrestler for his school, I thought.

"We're from down the street," Natalie said. "And these are our country mouse cousins from Liberty in to the see the big city."

"Do you like it?" he asked Claire and me.

I nodded.

"She has laryngitis," Claire said. "The cold, you know. We love it. We want to come to school here."

"Let me bring you some hot tea," he said to me. I smiled and nodded. He added, "Put a little honey in it, that'll help."

He went off for the tea and Claire poked me in the ribs. "I think he's flirting."

"Oh right," I whispered.

But he behaved in a totally different way than if he thought I was a boy. He'd probably have left me to think of the tea myself, or expect that the women around me would take care of me. Strange.

After lunch we figured we'd see a movie, a "chick flick." There was a new romantic comedy that Natalie and her mom both wanted to see, and they agreed that Natalie's dad would never care about having missed it, so we ended up with popcorn and Junior Mints in the dark theater.

"Hey," Claire said. "Scrunch down, I want to try something."

I scooted down in my seat, propping my feet against the seat in front of me and bending my knees. She sat up tall in her seat and put her arm over my shoulders. I rested my head back on her arm.

"This is cool," I whispered.

"I'm just checking it out," she said.

"You're great."

She shrugged. "I'm just me."

After the movie, we wandered, blinking, into the afternoon sunlight of the lobby. "Okay girls," Natalie's mom said, "time to go and put our secret agent back into deep cover so I can get you back to your parents before my credibility slips."

CHAPTER SEVENTEEN

CLAIRE

She couldn't help but steal a look at Chris from time to time on the drive back to Liberty. The transformation to Emily had been surprisingly effective. She was big for a girl, but as they walked through the mall and Claire looked around at other women, she realized that there was a heck of a lot of variety among women. She saw a few who were at least six feet tall, one who was well over two hundred pounds, another with eyebrows like caterpillars, women with huge butts, women with flat chests, women with chests bigger than Claire's butt, women who looked like models, women who looked like adolescent boys on purpose. There were women with big hands and feet, women with tiny hands, one woman in a wheelchair whose legs didn't work at all. Claire was glad that she got to date someone with all the right working limbs, and better yet, who actually looked good as either a boy or a girl. How many kids at her school could say that about their date?

She put her forehead against the cold window and let herself doze, feeling exhausted. In her dreams her own body shifted and changed, getting bigger and more spacious. When she woke with the car pulling into her own driveway, she felt bigger than usual, as if she extended outside her own skin.

She kissed Chris, who was still grinning, and scooped her bag out of the trunk. There was a lot more mystery in the world than she'd thought.

Her own bedroom looked different to her, as if she'd walked into a stranger's house. She spent a few minutes looking around. She didn't feel as solid as usual and instead of being alarmed, she thought that she could choose which pieces of this life she wanted back and which she wanted to let go. How many people got that opportunity?

She got out the T-shirt and sleeping shorts she wore to bed, but then paused in front of the full mirror by her closed door. She pulled off her shirt, bra, jeans and underpants and stood naked in front of the mirror. This was her. Maybe she wanted slightly larger breasts and worried that she'd put on weight on her butt when she was older, like her mom was starting to do, but there was no question in her mind that this body was right for her. She touched her arms, her belly and then her thighs.

What was the opposite of gender dysphoric? Gender euphoric?

Claire grinned at herself in the mirror. Yes, she was gender euphoric. She'd have to remember to tell Emily.

CHAPTER EIGHTEEN

I dropped Claire off at her house and drove home. Mom was helping Mikey with homework in the dining room, or rather standing over him and making sure he was actually doing it, and Dad was watching TV, so I sat down with him.

"How was the city?" he asked.

"Great," I said.

"Who's this other girl?" he asked.

"Just someone I met online who turned out to be cool. She's in my same grade." I added that last bit so he wouldn't think she was some kind of Internet pervert.

"You like her?" he asked.

"Sure," I said, then thought through the implications of that question. "Oh, you mean do I *like* her?"

He looked at me as if I'd lost a few brain cells.

"Dad, if I was cheating on Claire, I wouldn't take her along, would I? Natalie's just cool. She's from Chicago."

He made some grumbles of agreement and settled back into the couch. "How's that other problem?"

I had to roll back the movie in my head to recall what he was talking about. Right, my alleged impotence. "It's fine," I said. "I'm doing good."

"Good," he said.

That was it with the questions. My dad was funny that way. He'd have these spurts of concern and the rest of the time it was like the family was made up of supporting characters in the drama of his job and the cars.

I watched TV with him for a while and then went upstairs to lie in bed and relive the day over and over again. For so long I'd thought I was trapped in this life and now I could see the way out and I knew I could take it. Now it was just a matter of moving through the obstacles. My next milestone was set for my appointment with Dr. Mendel on Thursday.

***

"You said I should come up with a plan," I told her. "I want a plan."

"Good," she said. "I think you probably already have one, you just haven't thought it through or formalized it."

She was right, and I told her how I planned to work all summer and as much as I could for the next few years, and to go to community college until I could get the money together for the physical transformations that I wanted.

"What about hormones?" she asked. "Are you still taking the ones you got illicitly?"

"Yes."

"We need to get you to an endocrinologist and do this right. We need a plan for talking to your parents."

I sighed. "It's going to suck," I said.

"Do you want to do it here?" she asked.

"You're brave."

She smiled. "It's my job."

"Yes," I said with tremendous relief. "I do want to tell them here." It was so good not to be in this all by myself anymore.

"Okay, let's talk about when you feel you'll be ready."

I liked that she left it up to me to decide. It was late March now with spring break coming up next week and the potential for a few more trips to see Natalie. I didn't want to risk losing that. Then I was in the crunch to the end of the school year.

"Can we do it in June?" I asked.

"Sounds like a good time to me. What are you going to do at home between now and then?"

"Be a good boy," I offered, raising my eyebrows at her.

She laughed.

I was a good boy at home, actually, and it seemed so much easier now that I could get out of the boy role with Claire and Natalie and Dr. Mendel. Playing the good boy now felt like a really long dress rehearsal for a play I would never star in. Mom commented about how great it was that my visits with Dr. Mendel were helping and I agreed happily.

I made an offer to Dad to help him sell some of his used car parts on eBay if I got a cut, and I even managed to play with Mikey a couple times. He was always making up these games in which superheroes from his favorite cartoons had to fight each other, and he never minded that I took the women heroes for my characters.

***

My birthday isn't my favorite time of year. It's near the end of April, so the world outside is slushy. At least that smell of hope is in the air, gently warm and green, and every year I let myself hope it's going to be different than the year I got a tool box, or the model car, or the neckties, the suit jackets, and so on. I used to hope I'd get gifts I wanted, but now I just hope I won't get anything too awful. I asked for a couple of computer games and for a copy of some graphic design software to practice with in case I ever want my own website.

Mom asked if I wanted a party, but I said not really, so she suggested we all go out to dinner, the family and Claire and one of Mikey's friends. That didn't sound like a particularly fun evening to me, so I added, "Can I invite Natalie and her mom?"

They were more than happy to come out for my birthday, but by the time the evening rolled around, I was regretting my invitation. We had only one nice restaurant in town and I picked that because I didn't want to have to drive too far with my family, and I thought it would be fun for Natalie to see downtown Liberty in all its glory. But when we pulled up in front of DaVinci's, I wanted to turn around and head home. The restaurant looked very small and kitschy compared to those in the big malls in the cities. I worried that my family would be too strange and at the same time I worried they'd realize Natalie had been born a boy. This was shaping up to be the worst birthday ever.

Claire grabbed my elbow and dragged me into the red and gold waiting area where Natalie and her mother sat on a low, red velvet bench. Claire made the introductions because my mouth was too dry for me to talk effectively, and then we were all seated at a long, rectangular table. Mom quizzed Natalie's mom about what kind of law she practiced, which left Dad to interrogate Natalie.

"So, you're in the Cities?" was his first attempt.

"We moved from Chicago a couple of years ago. I'm a junior at Maple Grove," she said, deftly tearing off a piece of garlic bread with her manicured nails. I envied Natalie's hands. Her fingers tapered toward the tips, so even though she had wide hands, she still looked great with the long, thick manicured nails she wore. My hands were square the whole way, from the base of my palms to my blockish fingers. In long nails I would look like a drag queen.

"And how did you meet?" Dad continued, though I'd already told him.

"We met online," Natalie said. She knew he already knew, because Claire and I had prepped her thoroughly on what we'd told my parents. "Gaming. We've been playing together for, what, four months? And I just thought that Em—uh, Chris was really cool." She kept going, but Dad had heard it. And I'd heard it so now all the blood in my body was rushing to my head, making it feel like it would burst open. That wouldn't have been a bad way to go just then.

"What were you going to call Chris?" Dad asked.

"Amalia," Claire said. "It's one of Chris's characters. Sometimes we get so caught up in the game, we call each other by those names even when we're hanging out together. My character name is Vaorlea."

"The Mighty," I added reflexively, though my voice came out as a squeak.

"You play a girl?" Dad asked me.

I nodded.

"Most mages are girls," Claire lied. "Natalie plays a guy because she's a barbarian. I mean, warrior."

That jab wasn't lost on Natalie, who flinched when Claire said it, but she went with the flow. "Yeah," she said with a pointed look at Claire. "It's kind of weird sometimes, having to be a guy. But it's also kind of cool to see how differently people respond to you. It's an expanding experience."

"But you're a girl," Dad said to Claire, meaning in the world of the game, though he didn't say that.

"The whole time," she said, trying not to smirk. "But my character is a paladin so she also uses magic. I'm not a barbarian like Natalie." She paused and shot another glare at Natalie.

Natalie coughed quietly into her napkin, and I couldn't tell if she was embarrassed or trying not to laugh. Probably both.

Claire continued, "You get bonuses and stuff. Chris's character is very powerful. He can wipe out a whole tribe of orcs with his flamestrike. Well, it's not just that, he's also got these dots...that's damage over time spells. One of them makes the monster explode..."

She trailed off as Dad's eyes glazed over. Claire often said that the quickest way to get parents off a topic was to start going on about gaming.

Mom changed the topic by asking Natalie's mom about their house, and Natalie glared at Claire, "A barbarian, huh?"

"You're just lucky his magic user is named Amalia," she shot back in a deadly whisper. They were sitting next to each other, both facing me, while Dad was on my left, so I barely heard what they said to each other.

Natalie looked at me wide-eyed. "I'm so sorry," she mouthed.

I shook my head because I didn't trust my voice entirely yet. The inside of my skin felt like Jell-O still quivering. I tried to eat some spaghetti, but my throat was so tight it hurt to swallow. I wanted my mom and dad to know and understand so badly, but how could I survive telling them if I got this nervous about one slip?

The rest of dinner passed uneventfully, except for Mikey and his friend, John, trying to throw meatballs at each other. We dropped off Claire, and Mom gushed the rest of the way home about how smart Natalie's mom was. But when we got home, Mom took me aside in the kitchen.

"They're very nice," she said. "But I'm not sure you should go into the Cities to see Natalie alone."

"Why not?"

"I think Claire's jealous of her," Mom said. She called to my dad, who was still taking his boots off in the entryway, "Jerry, don't you think Claire's a little jealous of Natalie?"

"Yep," he shouted back. A minute later he stood in the kitchen entrance. "There was something going on between those two. That Natalie's an attractive girl."

Mom nodded. "And she has a great way with her makeup. Most girls her age either don't wear any or they put on way too much or, well, all that dark eyeliner isn't doing anything for Claire's complexion. Natalie is tasteful. But if you like Claire better, you need to let her know that. She's probably feeling threatened."

"And maybe you should try being a barbarian for a while," Dad added on his way to the garage.

Mom looked at me quizzically because she'd missed that part of the conversation, but I just shook my head.

"You and Claire have been dating for awhile," she said. "Is it serious?"

"Yeah, I guess so."

"I remember when I was dating your father in high school," she said with a smile that made her face look young and wistful. "Some of the other girls thought I shouldn't just stick with one guy. Do you get that?"

"Some. Other guys on the swim team date around more, but I don't really want to."

She put her hand gently on my upper arm. "You don't have to do anything you don't want to, honey. I just want you to have someone that you love. Someday I'll get to come visit you in a nice house with your children and your wife, and whoever that is, I hope she makes you very happy."

I wondered if she had too much wine at dinner. I think she was trying to let me know that it was okay to dump Claire for Natalie, or not, whichever I wanted. As long as I got married and had kids. At least that's how it sounded to me because all I could see was this picture in her mind of me growing up like her, or rather like Dad.

"Sure," I said.

"You're going to make some woman very happy some day," she added.

I managed a smile. "I hope so."

I went upstairs to send Natalie an email about my parents' compliments to her. I also wondered about what they'd said about Claire. I wasn't attracted to Natalie at all, but I don't think I'd ever said that out loud. Maybe I should do something nice for Claire. She took such good care of me, and she'd saved my butt at dinner.

CHAPTER NINETEEN

CLAIRE

"Let me take you out to dinner tonight," Chris said over the phone. Claire looked at the stack of books next to her computer. She wasn't going to get through all of them tonight anyway and it was a Saturday. Plus she had Monday off for Memorial Day, so she had two more full days to finish that paper for AP English.

"Where?" she asked.

"How about the new seafood place?"

"It's going to be packed."

"We'll go early and then see a movie or something."

Claire smiled into the phone. "Are you asking me out on a date?"

"You *are* my girlfriend," he said but there was a strained sound in his voice.

They set a time for him to pick her up and Claire hung up wondering if he was upset that they hadn't seen as much of each other the last three weeks. Claire knew her house was a refuge for Emily and that not getting to come over as often she once did probably sucked for her…him…her?

She rolled her neck and stood up from the desk. How Chris kept her identity straight all those years was amazing. Now that she'd started to see the outline of Emily inside of Chris, Claire found names and pronouns colliding in her head all the time. She wanted to just think "Emily" and "she" all the time to get herself used to it and to honor the person Emily was—but they spent so much time together at school and in places where people could overhear them, that she had to keep saying "Chris" and "he." But the more she said that, the more her brain reverted back to think of Emily as Chris.

So try harder, she told herself. Emily deserved to be acknowledged as a full person in her own right and Claire resolved again to manage that without making a stupid slipup like Natalie had at the birthday dinner. Natalie of all people, Claire thought, should have known better. But, maybe getting to transition young had made her careless now.

Emily and Natalie had been hanging out more while Claire was busy with the yearbook committee and all her classes. Of course Emily had plenty of schoolwork too, but she hadn't taken as many AP courses as Claire because she wasn't aiming for a top college. She would eventually end up spending more money on surgeries than most kids took out in student loans. While Claire toiled away at home, she covered for Emily's trips into the Cities to hang out with Natalie and go to the support group. She and Emily still got together at least once a week and they exchanged notes in school every day. Claire really wished Emily would shell out for some kind of mobile device so that she could just text her.

Claire hopped in the shower and afterward stood for a while in front of the bathroom mirror looking at her own face. In the last two months, she'd learned more about makeup than she ever imagined she would—including the fact that a little bit of indigo eye shadow really brought out the gold tints in her hazel eyes. When she watched women like her mother who put on makeup religiously to be more attractive to men, it scared her. She never wanted to feel like she needed a man so much that she'd add all that mirror time to her day.

But when she watched Emily and Natalie, a whole new view opened up to her. For them being beautiful wasn't a burden, it was a self-expression they were willing to fight for. Their feminine beauty was the battle standard for claiming their own identity. She had never realized that femininity could be a radical act because she'd never seen a feminine woman as strong in her identity as Emily or Natalie, or even Natalie's mother.

Now that she knew what powerful beauty looked like, she noticed it in other women all over the place. Her English teacher also had it and wore her makeup like warpaint that made her dark skin and eyes gently grab and hold the attention of anyone looking at her.

Claire drew thin black lines around her eyes and then brushed on the shimmering tan eye shadow under her brows and the indigo color on her eyelids the way the girls had taught her. Foundation and blush were too much still, but she chose a pink lip gloss from the basket full of the cosmetics her mom kept bringing home and applied that. She picked small silver hoop earrings and then crossed the hall to riffle through her closet until she found a blue-gray shirt with a cute collar to wear with her black skirt.

"Oh my God," her mom said from the kitchen when she saw Claire. She stopped scrubbing the countertop and straightened up. "What have you done with my daughter?"

"Chris is taking me out to dinner," she said. "Are you going out later? Can we watch a movie here afterward?"

"I'll probably be home at ten, if that's not too early for you," her mom said with the slightly patronizing lilt that reminded

Claire she didn't have a choice. She added, "I think Chris is a good influence on you."

"I know he is," Claire said with a grin.

When he arrived to pick her up, Chris's response was almost as surprised as her mom's. He blinked a few times and then closed his eyes tight for a second and opened them.

"Are you wearing blue? And eye shadow?"

"Yep. Come on, drive. I don't want to have to wait in line forever."

He pulled the car out of her driveway and headed for the seafood place.

Claire rested her hand on his leg just above the knee. "When I see how hard you have to fight to get to wear makeup … it made me realize that it's not just about being some stupid girlie girl."

"Well…" Chris said and laughed.

"Oh you know what I mean."

They beat the dinner crowd and got a quiet table off to one side of the main dining room where they proceeded to eat an obscene amount of crab, clams, shrimp and butter.

"Did you want to catch a movie?" Chris asked as Claire was leaning back in her chair and cradling her overstuffed belly in her hands.

"Let's go watch one at my house. Mom's out for a while, and I like when we don't have a bunch of other people around." She didn't add that she wanted to make sure she didn't have to fight Chris about who was paying for the movie. He'd already dropped plenty of money on her with this dinner, and she knew how much he needed to save it all.

"Thank you," she added. "This was perfect. Apparently I needed to consume a pound of protein covered in butter."

He laughed. "It's for how sweet you've been. And I wanted us to have a real date again."

"Real dates are nice," Claire said.

He smiled, but she saw a flash of tension around his eyes.

"What are you worried about?" she asked.

He shook his head and paid the bill. When they were outside in the car with the sweet spring air rolling in the open windows he asked, "Are we going to end up just really good friends?"

"I'm not planning on it," Claire said.

"You don't kiss me like you used to."

"We've had a lot going on!" she protested.

That wasn't a good enough reason, she realized. She looked around the parking lot. People were walking to and from the restaurant, but they weren't paying attention to the cars. She climbed awkwardly as far into Chris' lap as she could get and kissed him hard. His arms came up around her with a tight desperation as their lips met.

When they broke apart, his eyes were still questioning her. She carefully got back into her seat.

"My house," she said.

It was still early in the evening. The sun was low over the houses, but wouldn't set for a while yet. Her mom's car was out of the garage, and Claire figured they had at least two hours until they could expect her home. She took Emily's hand and pulled her through the living room toward the bathroom. "I'm picking the movie," she said. "You do the makeup."

"What?"

"Put some on, I'm serious."

She flicked on the TV and started flipping though the On Demand movies, though she really didn't care what they watched. Something shallow so they didn't have to pay attention to it.

Emily came out a few minutes later with a light touch of makeup around her eyes, solid foundation, a hint of blush and a lip shimmer. She'd fluffed her hair as much as she could, but it was still too short. Her jeans and sweater were gender neutral enough to work either way.

Claire beckoned her to the couch. If she'd thought this through, she realized, she could have cued up "I Kissed a Girl" on the iPod speakers. When Emily sat, she leaned forward and gently traced the side of her face. She didn't know what to say, or to expect, so she just kissed her.

It wasn't radically different from every other kiss they'd shared. Emily's lips were big, soft and familiar and the presence of lip shimmer just made the kiss a little sticky.

Claire pulled back. "Okay, this is silly."

"What?"

She hopped up and got tissues and makeup wipes. "The other girl I kissed wasn't wearing anything on her lips and my lip gloss on your shimmer is just yucky."

Emily laughed and wiped off her lips. Then she took the makeup wipes and removed the rest of it.

"You might be trying too hard," she said.

"All the time," Claire said as she wiped off the makeup around her eyes.

"Movie?" Emily asked.

Claire kissed her. This time no yucky lip gloss got in the way. For the first few minutes of making out, part of Claire's mind stood apart from the experience, waiting to see if anything felt new in a bad way. Emily smelled sweeter than the Chris that Claire was used to and her kisses felt more tentative, but that was easy to understand.

Claire's favorite parts of the experience hadn't changed. She still loved the feel of strong hands on her back, and it didn't matter if those were male or female. She appreciated being kissed carefully and thoughtfully. And she loved the feeling of melting into another human being whom she cared about. She let her whole mind dissolve into that experience.

CHAPTER TWENTY

After a couple of quiet months, the big day was coming. I'd gone back and forth about it, but I solidified my resolve when I ran out of hormones in May. Taken at half the prescribed dose, the bottle Natalie gave me lasted two months. Even at that low dose, I felt a difference in myself. First I wasn't so angry all the time and on the darkest days, the fierce edge of the blackness seemed to dull. More exciting was the fact that my skin softened all over my body. As I let the hair grow back in on my arms, it seemed lighter than it had been. I could begin to understand how much my body would change in this process, how I really could stop being a man altogether and become the woman I knew myself to be.

I told Mom and Dad that I had something I wanted to talk to them about and asked them to come see Dr. Mendel with me that Thursday. They looked alarmed, but agreed to come with me when I refused to say more. Dr. Mendel said she'd set aside a couple hours in case it took longer than our regular session to talk to them. I had stashed a few books at her office the week before that I thought would help them understand.

I was so nervous on the way over that I couldn't sit still.

"I don't know why we have to do this in her office," Mom complained. "Why can't you just tell us?"

"It's okay," I said for the hundredth time. "It's just easier this way."

"Did you get Claire pregnant?" she asked, apparently her worst fear.

"No, Mom, we're not having sex, honest."

I willed the car to move faster, though my dad was a speedy driver to begin with. At the same time, I wondered how long it would take mom to get to the right question. I worked out the math in my head. She was asking a question about every ninety seconds, which was about 960 questions a day, except that we'd need time to eat and sleep, so let's assume 480 questions a day, or 2,880 questions a week with Sunday off, would that be enough for her to get around to asking if I was really a girl in a single week? Probably not.

"Are you sick?" she asked.

"No, Mom."

"But you needed an appointment to tell us about this?"

"Yes."

We finally pulled into the parking lot, and I ushered them through the doors and into the lobby. I almost knocked on Dr. Mendel's door I was so eager to get this over with, but she opened it less than a minute after we rounded the corner.

"Come in," she said. "Mr. and Mrs. Hesse, it's good of you to come today. Please have a seat."

Mom and Dad sat on the couch, so I took the comfy chair on the end and Dr. Mendel sat in her usual spot facing the couch.

Everyone in the room had dressed up for this appointment. I'd put on my darker jeans and a light blue button-down shirt. Mom was in one of her work outfits with slacks and a V-neck sweater that made her look younger and pretty. She even had on earrings and makeup, though she'd been home from work long enough to take them off if she wanted to. Cleaned up from his construction outfit, Dad wore khakis and a long-sleeved pullover shirt with a collar. And Dr. Mendel was actually in a long, gray knit dress with pearls looping down over her ample bosom and hanging in delicate silver drips from her ears. I was betting she dressed more stereotypically female so that she'd have more authority with my parents about gender-related topics.

I tried to take a deep breath, but my chest wouldn't really expand, so the attempt ended up long and shallow. Okay, what was the worst that could happen? They could throw me out. I had turned seventeen in April, so I was almost old enough to make all my own decisions legally. I could probably stay at Claire's for a while and finish school, or at least that was a nice fantasy. I'd hold on to that one.

"Chris," Dr. Mendel said as if introducing me. We agreed that I had to tell them, rather than her. She was there for support, but I had to do this.

"Um," I said, rather inelegantly. "Thanks for coming. So, ah. Well, I don't really know how to say this so if it comes out funny I hope you'll just hear me out. It might not make a lot of sense right away, but I think with time it will make a whole lot of sense."

"You're gay," Mom blurted out.

"I'm a girl," I said.

Dead silence.

"No, you're not," Mom said.

"Yes, I am."

"Christopher," she said in her low pitched warning tone.

"Ever since I can remember, I've known I was a girl," I said, looking back and forth between them and my hands. Dad's eyebrows were both tilting out at angles, and Mom's mouth disappeared into a thin line. "When I was little I tried to hang out with the other girls, but everyone said I was a boy and so eventually I just played along, but I've always known I was a girl."

"No you're not," Mom said. "You are very clearly not a girl." She turned toward Dr. Mendel and demanded, "What on earth have you been telling him?"

Dr. Mendel remained silent while I took another long, shallow breath. "Mom," I said as firmly as I could manage. "There's a condition called transsexualism where a kid gets born with the brain of the opposite sex. That means that although I have a boy's body, inside I really am a girl."

"So you like to wear dresses?" Dad asked. He looked confused and incredulous. His normally tanned face was as pale as parchment.

"Well sort of," I said. "But that's not the point. The point is that I feel like a woman inside, and I want the hormones and surgery so I can live my life as a woman."

"Oh," he said. "Oh God."

The room fell silent.

From where it rested on his thigh, Dad's right hand twitched open and closed. Dr. Mendel sat like a rock and watched them while I shifted in my chair and failed to find a position where I felt like I wasn't about to get hit by lightning.

"If this is a joke…" Mom started.

"Mrs. Hesse, it's not a joke," Dr. Mendel spoke up. "Your child has a rare but treatable condition. I think you've noticed that as Chris is more self-expressed, there's a corresponding rise in happiness."

I noticed that she was very diplomatically avoiding any pronouns in her statements, which I appreciated. At this point I think female pronouns would have sent my mom through the roof, and male pronouns would have made me feel like crap. Yeah, I had a good doctor.

"Chris is a boy," Mom said. She sat back against the couch and folded her arms tightly against her chest. Her eyes narrowed to hostile slits. "He just needs to learn to live that way, not have his head filled with this nonsense."

Silence stretched out again until Mom stood up abruptly.

"We're leaving," she declared.

"No," I said. "We're not."

She looked at Dad to back her up. "Let's hear all of it," he said grimly as if he were talking about a list of war casualties.

Mom sat back down and crossed her arms again with her hands in fists. "All right, but I don't believe it."

"It's scientifically proven," I said. "And besides, what really matters is that when I get to be a girl, I feel like myself. All these years I've had to pretend to be someone I'm not." My voice rose. "Don't you want me to be happy?"

"Chris," Dr. Mendel warned before anyone else could answer. I tried to calm down. She was right, this was a bad time to ask leading questions of my parents before we brought them up to speed on the whole thing. She'd warned me last week that I'd had years to research this and they were probably hearing about it for the first time in their lives.

"Sorry," I offered.

Dr. Mendel picked up the conversation. "Sometimes a child is born whose internal sense of their gender does not match their external sexual characteristics, and in some cases, that difference is so pronounced that the child knows that he is the opposite sex from the body he was born with," she said in her grandmotherly tone. "It's called Gender Identity Disorder, or gender dysphoria. This is what happened for Chris. While everyone around assumed Chris was a boy, which is quite natural, inside Chris has always felt like a girl. There are thousands of people like Chris living in America, and most of them make a successful transition to the gender they feel inside and live the rest of their lives that way as productive, well-adjusted members of society.

"You brought Chris to therapy because you noticed, quite rightly, that your child was struggling with mood problems. The good news is that your child is actually very bright and socially well developed. Considering what Chris has had to live with, she is an outstanding individual. This is not about anything you did or didn't do. It's a biological condition determined before birth.

You have a child you can be proud of. Chris has been very strong in the face of considerable adversity and some of that is due to the values you've instilled. Now Chris needs your support, more than most kids do, to take the last few steps to adulthood."

Dr. Mendel sat back in her chair. I wanted to bottle that speech so I could listen to it every day for the next year or two.

"Are you done?" Mom asked coldly.

"Yes," Dr. Mendel said. "Though we have a few pamphlets and books for you to look at if you'd like."

Mom looked at me. "Anything else?"

I didn't know what to say. Her face looked like an ice sculpture. I was tempted to turn to Dr. Mendel and say "rescue me" but I figured that wouldn't help much.

Dad broke the silence. "There are other kids like this?" he asked Dr. Mendel.

"Yes," she said.

"How do they know?"

"There's a persistent sense of being the wrong gender that lasts for years, sometimes life-long. It's natural for children to be curious about the opposite sex, maybe even wonder what it's like, but I think you'll agree that having a persistent belief that you're a girl over ten years or more is something more than curiosity or a desire to avoid manhood."

He looked at me. "You always did cry a lot. I thought you were a sissy. But you toughened up."

"I've been pretending," I said.

"So you want to be a woman…does that mean you want to date guys?"

"No," I said. "Actually I still like girls better."

"Jesus Christ," he said and all but rolled his eyes. "That makes no sense at all." He picked up a pamphlet from the side table, stood up and crammed it into his pocket. "All right, I'm done with this. Chris, you coming with us?"

"Sure," I said and stood up with a wide-eyed look at Dr. Mendel.

"Would you two wait outside just for a minute?" she asked.

After a final glare from my mother at Dr. Mendel, they walked through the door and shut it loudly behind them.

"That sucked," I said.

"Give them time," she said. "They're going to go through stages. They're in shock right now, and then they'll be in denial for a while. Try not to let them blame themselves, and if they get too angry…if you're afraid, call me and get out of the house, okay?"

"Yes."

"Promise me you won't try to tough it out if it's more than you can handle."

"Okay," I said.

"You can do this," she told me. "You have me and Claire and Natalie, lots of people supporting you. Let your folks know that you love them and you're being honest with them."

I nodded and thanked her, then headed out the door. Mom and Dad were already in the car with the engine running.

When I got into the backseat, they didn't say anything at all or look at me; the silence held all the way home. When we walked in the air felt icy compared to the warmth outdoors, and it wasn't because of the air conditioning. Dad made a beeline for the garage.

Mom dropped her purse on the table with an angry clatter.

"What the hell are you trying to pull?" she yelled at me.

"It's the truth," I said.

"You want to be a *woman*? That's ridiculous. Look at you!"

Into the pause in the tirade Mikey yelled from the living room, "Fag!"

Mom turned toward him. "GO TO YOUR ROOM!" she screamed louder than I'd ever heard. He leaped to his feet and tore up the stairs.

She dropped her voice, which didn't help much because now it sounded like a butter knife trying to saw through bone. "Being a woman isn't going to solve anything," she said to me. "It's just going to make your life hell. Look at you, you'd make the ugliest woman I can imagine. You'd be a freak. You need to drop this bullshit right now, young man. I don't want to know what put this crazy idea in your head, but you are grounded until you come to your senses. No more computer, no more trips to the city, and I'm going to find another doctor for you. Now you go to your room too."

I ran for my room. I logged on to GenderPeace and quickly posted a message that my mom had lost it and I might not be able to get online in the near future. Then I sent Natalie a quick note, and an email to Claire saying I was going to need help.

Moments after I hit send, Mom threw the door open.

"Get off that," she said.

I stepped back. She yanked the cords out of the wall and picked up the whole computer, carrying it out of the room. A minute later she came back and took my phone. Then she slammed the door behind her.

I waited. The house was quiet. No, I could hear her in the garage yelling at Dad. Then him yelling back. I couldn't tell what he was saying and I thought about putting my ear to the floor, but I didn't really want to know. Instead I snuck out into the hall and tapped on Mikey's door.

"Yeah," he said softly.

"It's me."

He opened the door. His eyes were red and he sniffled a few times, trying not to cry. "I didn't mean it," he said almost in a whisper. "Why is Mom so mad?"

I shut the door behind me and sat on the edge of his bed. He had a Batman bedspread, though I'd heard Mom tell him he was getting too old for it. Right now he looked pretty young even for nine. His brown eyes were huge and red with the effort of not crying.

"Mom's not mad at you," I said. "She's mad at me."

He sat on the foot of the bed, one leg tucked up under his other leg, and idly rearranged the action figures beside him. "She said you want to be a girl?" he asked. "That's weird."

"Yeah," I said. "I do."

"Am I going to turn out like that too?" he asked.

I smiled. "No. I've always wanted to be a woman. You don't. You're a boy."

"I am," he said with gusto. "Girls are gross. I don't know why you want to be one. Does this mean you're going to turn into my sister?"

I tried to read his face to see if he was going to use this against me later, but his pale skin and tight lips looked genuinely scared and concerned. "In a few years."

"Can they really make you into a girl?" he asked. "I never heard of anything like that. What do they do?"

I didn't know how much to tell him, so I stuck to the basics. "It takes surgery and hormones. They don't just zap me with a laser."

He laughed a little, as I'd intended. "That would be a funny power to have. What would you call that superhero? Girl Man? I'd zap Zach, he deserves it."

He'd started to grin, and I smiled back. "I think maybe we should only turn people into girls who want to be girls," I warned. "Otherwise it's not fair."

"Yeah," he said. "Is Mom going to be mad at you for a long time?"

"Probably," I said.

"Can I have your car?"

"You can't drive for seven more years," I pointed out. "What would you do with it? Sit in the driveway?"

"It's cool."

"I still like cars," I told him.

"You're going to be a girl who likes cars?"

"Such creatures do exist," I told him.

"But you're still my brother right now, right?" he asked.

"Yeah."

"Want to play superheroes until Mom's not mad at you?"

I pretended to think about it. "Can I be the girls?" I asked.

"Yeah!" he said with emphasis. "I don't want 'em."

His favorite game these days was to compose teams of superheroes and explain how they pounded the crap out of each other. I picked my five favorite girl heroes and he picked an amalgam of men and aliens. We whaled on each other until Mom called us down for a very silent dinner.

CHAPTER TWENTY-ONE

A large vacuum invaded our house, which is to say: life sucked. Mom rescinded all my communication and travel privileges. She cancelled my appointments with Dr. Mendel and set one up with Dr. Webber. I refused to go. I was putting up with her other bullshit because I didn't want to find out if Claire's mom would really take me in if Mom threw me out, but there were a couple boundaries I was holding firm, and that was one.

We were at a standoff. I spent a lot of time working on cars with Dad who never brought up anything from the visit to Dr.

Mendel. I also played with Mikey a lot. My girl team even beat his men and aliens team a few times.

With permission, I managed one trip over to Claire's in late June, when she said she needed my geometry book, and told her what had happened. I stashed the duffel bag at her house. When I got home it was clear why Mom allowed me to visit Claire. She'd been through my room and taken my copies of Kate Bornstein's *Gender Outlaw*, Jenny Boylan's *She's Not There* and the volume of *True Selves* I was hoping she would read. She also took some of my X-men comics, which puzzled me, and the swimsuit issue of *Sports Illustrated*, which was actually Dad's but I had lifted it to imagine myself as those models.

My senior year of high school started in two months and then she wouldn't have so much control over my activities. I figured I could wait her out. After I talked to Dad about it, we set my computer up in the garage so I could keep selling his car bits on eBay. I still had a roof over my head and food, and I was making decent money with the eBay work, so I could wait a few months to have my girl-time back. Half the time Dad didn't pay any attention to what I was doing on the computer because he was under a car or deep in its engine. I'd open another browser window under the eBay window and post on GenderPeace. It was amazing to see so many people from all over the world offer support for my situation.

"Remember, it's a process," one post said. "It took me a while to realize that my parents had to go through all this mourning for the loss of their son. My mom was crying almost every day and I thought it was because she was so ashamed of me. But really she was trying to let go of her old idea of me. Then for a while I felt like I was the one who killed her son and that was awful. But now we can talk about it, and she actually asked if I would come home for a visit sometime this year. Hang in there and give them time!"

"I'm sorry she cut off your good therapist," another said. "Keep coming back here, you need all the support you can get right now. You can do this."

The only funny part of the whole dismal time was a surprise

visit from Claire. She brought me some of her science fiction novels and an English textbook that I didn't need. While we were sitting in the kitchen talking, because Mom said I couldn't have anyone in my room, Mom came in.

"Did he tell you why he's grounded?" she asked Claire.

She shrugged. "School stuff." She was lying. I had told her everything and she thought it was awful, but she had two years of drama club and she sensed an opportunity.

"He thinks he wants to be a girl," Mom said. "Isn't that disgusting?"

Claire's eyes got huge. "Oh my God!" she said. She turned to me. "How could you!? You said that was only a phase. Chris! I'm so embarrassed!" She stood up and ran out of the house.

"Claire!" I yelled, quite dramatically. I grabbed my car keys off the counter and glared at Mom. "Thanks. Thanks a lot!"

Claire was standing by the passenger side of the car, face in her hands, shoulders shaking. When I got closer to the car, I could hear her muffled laughter. I bundled her into the passenger seat. Her mother had dropped her off and was going to come get her in an hour, but I got into the driver's seat and peeled off. Mom could re-ground me later when I got home.

A couple blocks away I had to stop because I was laughing too hard to see straight. "That was priceless," I said.

"I hope it wasn't too mean," Claire said. "But I just couldn't stand her crap. Maybe she'll actually feel bad for once. How long do you think it's going to take for you to comfort me?"

"Few hours?" I suggested.

"Good, I'll call Mom and tell her not to pick me up. We can catch a movie. I've got liner and eye shadow in my pocket if you promise to wear shades."

"You're making me feel like a junkie," I said.

"You don't want it?" she teased.

I smiled. "You're wicked."

"Just what you need. Come on, let's go see something mind-numbing while I plot my next performance."

I had one thing I wanted to bring up with her, and I didn't

know how to say it. "Claire, would you talk to Natalie and see if there's a way you can order hormones for me? Natalie knows the right stuff, and I'll pay you back for all of it."

I could feel her looking at me, though my eyes were on the road ahead. "That's not legal is it?"

"No," I said. "But my parents aren't going to take me to a doctor and…I need them."

She took a deep breath. "Chris…Emily, it's not going to hurt you to wait a few more months…" She sounded like she was going to say more, but I'd pulled over a few blocks from the theater.

I put my head forward on the steering wheel and sobbed, all the tension of the past weeks at home and the awful things Mom had said, plus the hopelessness of running out of the one thing that was making a positive difference, it all came out of me in deep, dry sobbing, my fingers wrapped white-knuckled around the wheel.

Claire rubbed my back with her palm. "It's going to be okay, it's just a matter of time."

"I don't have time," I managed. "Seventeen years and every day is torture. I can feel this stupid testosterone masculinizing me. It's making me all rough and hairy. And now it's worse because Mom and Dad know and they're awful. And I'm so close. I just want to be normal…a normal woman."

She rested her cheek on my shoulder. "Honey, I'm not sure you should ever want to be normal. I'll talk to Natalie, but I can't promise anything. I'm not into illegal and no matter how crazy things are, you shouldn't be either."

I dug into my pocket for a tissue and blew my nose. "Thanks. I'm sorry."

"I worry about you," she said. "Maybe you should call the good doctor."

I shrugged. "Maybe."

***

I had tried being a good kid for three or four weeks, but Mom showed no signs of relenting. She glared at me a lot. In her softer moments, she'd compliment me on something I was wearing and say how nice it made my shoulders look, or how tall I was getting. I started avoiding her. For a few days here and there, I could lose myself in the work on the Bronco with Dad.

I also started staying up later and later at night. In the quiet, dark hours, I could feel like myself again. Even if I didn't have my computer, I could dream about going out as a woman. For hours at night I would lie awake in bed and go through every detail of the trip to the mall with Natalie and her mom, and the few shopping trips I'd had with Natalie in May, and then I'd build out from there, imagining myself with an apartment in Minneapolis and a job, and everyone would call me "ma'am" or "miss." I could wear my hair long, and my skin would feel soft, even softer than it had on Natalie's borrowed hormones.

I wrote a few stories in the back of my chemistry notebook about a girl named Emily. Mom didn't know my name, though I was sure she'd be furious if she found them. I just didn't care so much anymore.

Staying up late meant that I could sleep in later. Even after I woke up in the mornings, I didn't get out of bed until I was forced to either by having to pee, or someone knocking on my bedroom door. Most days I could stay in bed until nearly noon, and then I only had to navigate the hours between noon and ten, when Mom went to bed.

I thought I was holding myself together pretty well, though I was only existing day to day, waiting for the next and the next so that I could get back to school and eventually escape this house completely. Until the dinner.

The dinner was out at a fancy restaurant in the neighboring town. The financial planning firm Mom worked for hosted it as a summer bonus because the business was doing well. Only the older kids from the families were invited, so Mikey got to luck out of it and spend the night at a friend's house.

Mom insisted that we dress up for it and make a good impression. "That means a jacket and a tie," she told me.

I wore them. I didn't much care one way or the other. The body in the jacket didn't feel like mine anyway. In the restaurant, we sat at a table with one of Mom's bosses and his family, a wife and three girls.

Mom introduced me as, "Chris, our oldest son," which seemed excessive, but I let it go. She didn't.

"We're very proud of Chris," she slipped in later. "He got a letter in swimming this year. He likes distance swimming best, can you imagine that? Swimming a mile?"

"Really?" the oldest girl asked. She was about my age and pretty in that I-would-kill-to-have-her-brow-line style. Too blond for me to be attracted to her, but slender in a way that made me envy her waist.

"Yeah," I said, sounding like a Neanderthal.

"You two are about the same age," Mom pointed out the obvious. "Why don't you come over here so you can talk to each other." She actually got up and switched places with the blond girl.

I didn't know what on earth she thought she was doing, and if it hadn't been a dinner for her work, I would have gotten up and left. Also I didn't want to offend this girl who was clearly caught in the crossfire of our feud. I kept my hands in my lap because they'd started to shake with the effort of sitting still.

Betsy was the girl's name, and she had that same nervous habit of talking that Claire has. We made it through the entrée with her telling me all about her school activities and her sisters, without my having to give more than one-word answers.

When she started winding down, I asked, "Where'd you get that sweater?"

"Banana Republic," she said. "Do you like it?"

"It's great. I have a pair of pants from them, very soft," I told her.

"They have great stuff, don't they? I saw this white quilted jacket I wanted, but how would you ever keep something like that clean?"

I laughed a little with her. It felt good to laugh, and to have some girl talk.

"Your eye shadow looks really good," I said. "Is it MAC?"

"No, it's actually Mary Kay. Mom's a director, so I get all these free samples from her. You like it? I thought it was too blue."

"It brings out the light colors in your eyes, it looks good," I said. "Do you like Mary Kay products?"

"Well, I like the soaps and lotions best," she said. "They make my skin so soft. Feel this." She held out the back of her hand and I touched it. It was as soft as feathers, but without feeling fragile.

"That's amazing, I wish my skin felt like that."

She giggled. "I could do your hands sometime."

From across the table, Mom interjected, "Don't you two look cute together."

I glared at her. She made it sound like we were dating, but she knew I had a girlfriend. I realized Mom didn't like Claire even more than she let on. She'd rather have me with this blond Mary Kay girl than with my goth-haired, kohl-eye-linered best friend in the world.

My glare didn't stop Mom, she went on. "Did Chris tell you about how he restores cars with his father? He's very good with his hands, but he also gets good grades. Well rounded."

"No, Mom," I said. "We were talking about makeup."

Mom's mouth shut in a chiseled line. Luckily the youngest sister chimed in about how she wanted to wear makeup and no one noticed the deadly looks passing between Mom and me. She didn't let me forget that remark, though. As soon as we were in the car, she started in about it.

"Chris, I can't believe you said that at dinner. Talking about makeup, honestly. I just want to be able to take my family out to a simple dinner with my office and not be mortified by my own child. Can't you just give it up for one night? Do you have to be a freak all the time? I don't know why you want to stand out so much. Your dad and I have given you everything we had, and you persist in this…perversion of nature."

"Sharon," Dad said in his warning tone.

"Don't try to calm me down. Chris is a man, and the sooner he accepts that, the better. I don't know where he came up with this crazy idea, but I have raised him as a boy and he will never be anything other than a man." She raised her voice and glared over her shoulder. "Do you hear that? You're a man, no matter what anyone tells you. Just look at yourself. That's all you'll ever be."

Internally I wobbled on the razor edge of sanity. Dad pulled into the driveway and I opened the car door before he'd stopped. I had my keys in my hand and ran to the front door before anyone could follow me. I dashed through the doorway and up the stairs to my bedroom where I bolted the door behind me. Then, for good measure, I pushed my desk in front of the door, panting with the effort and my rage.

I tore off my jacket, tie and shirt and looked around for a way to destroy them. In my top desk drawer was a pair of scissors and a hunting knife Dad had given me last year. First I thought I should just cut off the parts of me that had Mom so convinced I was a man. I stood over the desk, bracing myself on my left hand while the knife quivered in my right. I couldn't. Even though I hated that part of myself, I couldn't attack my own body that way.

Instead I sat down on the edge of my bed in my slacks and cut the arms off my jacket. As soon as the scissors bit through the cloth, I started to feel a clear determination rising inside of my outrage. I took each arm and cut it into strips, then I cut off the collar and used the knife to rip the jacket to rags. I took apart the shirt the same way, and then snipped perpendicularly across the tie, so that it lay on the floor in one-inch wide pieces.

I stood up and stepped out of my pants, which came under the blade next. I was naked except for my briefs and those weren't coming off because I refused to confront what was underneath them. I opened my closet door and looked into the comforting darkness.

Dad knocked on my door. "Open up," he said.

"No," I told him.

"Don't make me break in there, you won't like it."

"The desk is in front of the door, I'd like to see you try," I shot back at him.

He raised his voice. "Chris, open the door."

"No," I said, and then more loudly, "No!" I was screaming now as loud as I could, defying all the bullshit they'd put me through, "*No! No! No!*"

Leaning over the desk, I punched the door. I heard Dad step back from the other side, but it barely registered over my own shouting and hitting the door again with my fist.

I screamed, "No!" and hit the door again, harder, over and over again.

I saw blood on the door and heard my voice go hoarse from screaming, but I couldn't stop. The fury drove through me into the wood as I hit it. Only when my knuckle scraped the edge of the deadbolt and tore off a half-inch of skin did the pain slice through my rage.

I grabbed my right hand with my left and staggered into my closet to curl up in the clothes I'd dragged off their hangers. I was crying so hard I thought I was going to puke.

A booming impact hit the door so hard from the other side that the wood around the hinges groaned. Then twice more until wood splintered and the lock tore loose. I heard the scrape of the desk being pushed back and then Dad was kneeling down in the doorway to the closet. He grabbed my bloody hands and turned them palm up. He was afraid I'd slit my wrists, I realized.

"Didn't...cut...myself," I managed through my heaving breath. "Knuckles."

"Ah Chris," he said and closed his hand over the back of my neck. He gave me a tiny shake. "Jesus."

He got up and left. I curled deeper into the clothes pile, wishing it would all just go away. My head felt crushed. My eyes and sinuses burned with a damp fire.

Dad came back a few minutes later. I was still crying, but

not so hard. Now the tears just rolled down my face whether I tried to stop them or not. Dad had a stack of washcloths, bandage pads, tape and a bag of ice that he put on my right knuckles once he had a washcloth in place to stop the blood. He cleaned up my left hand and then very carefully ran a damp cloth over the right.

"Shit," was the one word he said during this process. He opened a couple of sterile bandage pads, pressed them over the knuckles and taped them loosely.

Then he helped me pull one of his baggy sweatshirts down over my head. I didn't realize how cold I was until he put the shirt on me. Then I started shivering uncontrollably.

He looped an arm under my shoulders and helped me across the room to my bed. Dragging my desk chair across the room, he sat next to the bed and put the ice pack on my bandaged hand. I struggled to come up with words but before any came I fell into an exhausted sleep.

CHAPTER TWENTY-TWO

When I woke up in the late morning, my right hand had a swollen lump that joined the knuckles together in a puffy, blue-purple mass. As loose as the tape was on the bandage, it still strained from the swelling. I gingerly pulled up one edge and peeked underneath. A line of scabs crossed my knuckles where the skin had split and torn, and most of the skin that should have been on my middle knuckle was gone, leaving a raw, red patch.

It hurt with both throbbing and burning pain, and I couldn't close my hand completely. I went and stood in the shower for a long time, holding the bandage out from the spray and wondering if I could just leave home. I could get in my car and drive to the

Cities and find a job doing something stupid, but I'd just be a kid from the sticks with no high school diploma.

Back in my room I put on jeans and a T-shirt and then listened to the sounds of the house, trying to figure out where my parents were. I was hungry enough to feel my stomach growl, but not hungry enough to walk into the kitchen if Mom was there. I noticed that Dad had cleared out the remnants of my torn up clothes from the night before. The bolt that I used on my door had been torn out of the molding, leaving two ragged holes where the screws had been. The casing for the bolt, which had been screwed into the molding, was still on the end of the bolt, hanging at a ridiculous angle. I pulled it off and pushed the bolt back along the door.

My parents weren't making any of their usual Sunday noises. After ten minutes I began to worry that they were sitting in the kitchen waiting for me to come down. I wasn't going to give them the satisfaction. I'd starve myself first. I lay back on my bed and folded my left hand behind my head, staring up at the white ceiling.

After a while, Dad's footsteps came up the stairs, heavy and slow. He knocked on my door. "Chris?"

"Yeah," I said.

He pushed the door open. "You coming downstairs so we can talk?"

I shrugged. "Is Mom going to rail on me again?"

"No," he said.

He sounded so tired that I sat up and looked at him. His jeans and shirt were as wrinkled as if he'd slept in them, and his face was deeply lined, eyes sunken and dark.

"Okay." I stood up more because of his face than what he said. I cared about him, and I felt a little afraid of him, but today he looked as beat up as I felt, so I figured I'd stick with him, at least until things got ugly.

I followed him downstairs and into the kitchen. Mom was sitting at the table, hands wrapped white-knuckle tight around a cup of coffee. If I decided to spend the rest of the day in my room, this would be my one chance today to eat something. I got myself a bowl of cereal before sitting down at the far end of the table, away from Mom. She looked at Dad.

"We think you should go see someone again," he said slowly. "Someone who can help you."

"You're the ones who stopped the visits with Dr. Mendel," I pointed out.

"We want you to go back to Dr. Webber," he said.

If I hadn't cried myself out the night before, I might have started yelling at them about what a jerk he was. But I still felt tired and worn out, and I wanted to know my options. I had nothing left to lose here and if it didn't get better fast, I was leaving.

"What's in it for me?" I asked.

"A chance to be well," Dad said.

I rolled my eyes. "I know what's wrong with me. That is not going to make me well."

Mom sighed. "Honey, would you just try to have an open mind? Maybe you're wrong about all this, have you thought of that?"

"What if I'm not? How long are you going to make me prove myself?"

They looked at each other. Dad shook his head slightly, Mom frowned. "What is it you want?" she asked.

This was clearly not the time to bring up surgery or going out dressed as a woman. "I want to see an endocrinologist, to go on hormone therapy," I said.

"What is that?" Mom asked.

"It's part of the process of transition…to a woman," I said. She opened her mouth, but I said, "Just listen. I'd start taking hormones for a year or two and the effects are reversible. If it turns out I'm wrong, I can just stop." I wanted to tell them how much better I felt when I was taking the hormones, more like myself and in charge of my life, less angry and hopeless. But then I'd have to admit I'd been taking someone else's prescription and that would get both me and Natalie in trouble.

"You want to take women's hormones?" Mom asked, her voice rising sharply at the end.

"You will when you hit menopause," I said. "Lots of people take hormones."

"I'm a woman," she said harshly.

"So am I," I shot back.

The three of us fell into another cold silence. I wondered where they'd stashed Mikey and if he was going to pop out of the other room at any moment and shout "fag" at me or if he was upstairs again trying not to cry. Then it occurred to me that they must have left him over at his friend's house so they could have this talk with their unfortunate son.

"All right, look," Dad said abruptly as he stood up from the table. He put his palms on the tabletop and leaned in toward both of us. "I'm no good at this shit and I'm sick of it. Chris, you're going to see Dr. Webber for the next month, and Sharon you go with him if you want. At the end of August if you still want to go, I'll take you to a hormone doctor and we'll see what he says. I don't want to hear any more about this."

He stalked away from the kitchen and a moment later the slam of the garage door echoed through the silent house.

Mom stood up and went upstairs. I washed my cereal bowl, dried it and put it back in the cupboard so it looked like I'd never been in the kitchen. Then I put on my coat and boots and left. Let Mom tell me later if I was still grounded.

I drove around for a while and then went to the public library to update my friends online about everything that had happened. I wanted to see Claire, but I was afraid that when I did, I'd just start crying again. I sent her an email instead. Then I went home to a very quiet dinner.

Monday morning, Mom and Dad went off to work as usual. I watched Mikey in the early part of the day, but then he went over to a friend's house. I drove to the nearest Home Depot, which wasn't all that near, and bought a new piece of molding for my doorframe. Then I went over to Claire's house. She put her arms around me as soon as she saw me in the doorway and dragged me to the couch. She didn't let go for about three hours.

***

Mom got us in with Dr. Webber as soon as possible. It was only two days later that I took a short, silent car ride to his office. She said she wanted to come in with me, so we ended up in that dreary office, with her on the couch and me in a chair. I sat back, crossed my arms and waited to hear what he was going to say. His hair was still closely cropped and perfectly done as if it hadn't grown at all since the last time I saw him six months ago. He looked like an actor playing the part of a psychiatrist in a commercial for an antidepressant.

"Chris, I hear things have gotten worse since I saw you last," he said with a slight, tense smile.

Now that I hadn't been to Dr. Webber in months I saw him differently, even through my anger. On the surface he looked so perfect from his distinguished graying temples and close trimmed nails to his sharply creased pants. But the overly tense way he sat in his chair made him always off balance. Dr. Mendel actually sat up straight and relaxed at the same time. I never saw her try to sit up straight, she just did it. Dr. Webber swayed and caught himself, straightened up and shifted his shoulders into place.

"Actually, things got better for a long time, and then my parents freaked out, and since then it's pretty much sucked," I told him.

Mom sighed loudly. "He wants to be a woman," she said.

Dr. Webber turned his chair more fully toward me and leaned forward. "Is that true?"

"Close," I said. "Actually, I am a woman, on the inside. I'd like my body to match my internal sense of myself."

"How do you know you're a woman?" he asked.

"How do you know you're a man?" I asked back. "It's a

feeling you have, a sense of yourself. I've just always known I was a woman—or a girl, when I was a kid—and I was confused about why everyone always stuck me with the boys."

He swiveled his chair back toward my mom and this started another sway, shift, straighten sequence. "Did you notice effeminate behavior in Chris when he was younger?"

"No," Mom said, "not really. He's always liked cars and girls and adventure games. He likes being outside a lot, and he's been on the swim team since he started high school."

"Chris, when did you start thinking you wanted to be a girl?" the doctor asked.

"I didn't start thinking it one day. Actually, what I remember is being surprised that other people didn't treat me like a girl. Mom, remember in first grade when I wanted a girl's name?"

"Aha!" Dr. Webber said. His hands pushed down on the seat of his chair, popping him up even straighter. "How old were you then, five, six? What was going on in the home at that time?"

That second question was directed to Mom who gave him a half shrug and raised her eyebrows. "I'm not sure I can remember."

"Was there any instability in the home?"

"I'm sure there was some. Money was really tight. I'd just taken a job, my husband was out of work for a while."

"Interesting," he said. "Well, Chris, I think we can work on this. I suspect what happened is that you've idealized women and degraded men, probably having to do with that stressful time in your early childhood. You saw your mother as capable and your father as helpless and decided it's better to be a woman. You may also have had some trouble bonding appropriately with your father and decided that you wouldn't make a good man. What we need to do is to rewire these patterns."

I sat very still and tried hard not to roll my eyes. He went on, "I'm going to come up with a treatment plan for you. Now what is important for you to understand is that this problem of yours is not physical, although it may seem that way, it is psychological. To attempt to treat it physically, is to go in the wrong direction. You can take hormones and get plastic surgery, but a 'sex change' is a misnomer. You will never be able to change your biological sex. You need to think about what kind of person you really want to grow up to be."

He turned his awful attention toward my mother. "You and your husband need to set a good example for Chris of a well-balanced marriage with strong masculine and feminine poles. I'd like the two of you to come see me, and I'd like Chris to come see me on his own next week."

Mom said something in agreement and thanked him. I wasn't listening. I hated him with a black, hopeless rage.

"See," Mom said when we got in the car. "He believes you can be cured psychologically. You don't need to go through all this craziness to become a woman. You can be fine the way you are."

"Mom," I said, letting out the words that came to my mouth without censoring them for once. "If I can't be a woman, I'd rather just die."

"Chris, don't talk that way! My God, you're just trying to shock me, aren't you?"

"No, I'm not. Just forget it. I'm going over to Claire's."

As soon as we got home, I drove over to her house and told her all about it. She said what a jerk he was a few dozen times, but was surprisingly quiet for Claire. Her eyes had a hard, dark look to them.

"I'll hurt him if I have to," she said at last. "I don't know how, but I'll find a way if he keeps treating you like that."

I felt comforted, and a little scared. Claire was scrappy and had a healthy disrespect for authority, but I didn't want her to get herself into serious trouble over me.

By the next week, I was ready to change my mind on that last point. Mom had basically lifted the social restrictions on my grounding. Mom and Dad went to see Dr. Webber and after they came home, we started having family dinners together every night where Mom would try to get Dad to talk about his day and Mikey would interrupt every two minutes with a story from school or a TV show he'd seen.

I confronted Dr. Webber about it when I was back in his office. "Do you really think all that family dinner stuff is going to make a difference?" I asked.

"I understand that you have a lot to be angry about," he said. "But you have to understand that people can change. Your parents can change and you can change. Now, Chris, I have a delicate subject to bring up with you, and that's your sexuality."

"Yeah, what about it?"

"Your mother tells me you have a girlfriend."

"Yeah."

"Are you sexual with her?" he asked.

"We make out and stuff, we haven't had sex. Why?"

"But you enjoy it?"

"Yeah," I said. "I love Claire."

"Then why would you want to be a woman? Don't you understand you'll become a lesbian?"

I must have stared at him for a whole minute before I could get my incredulous lips to move. "Look, Dr. Webber, do you think I'm stupid or something? Of course I know that. Do you think I haven't thought this whole thing through, over and over again? Do you think it's just a whim or something?"

"What do you think of when you think about being a woman?" he asked.

"I think about going to school," I said. "Same as now, except I'm a girl."

"Do you think about going into the girls' locker room? Looking at the other girls?" he asked.

"Not particularly."

"But you think about yourself, dressed as a girl. Do you ever find that arousing?"

I shrugged. There was no way I was touching that land mine.

"There is a condition that some people develop which causes them to be turned on by the idea of themselves in the clothing of the opposite sex, or even having a body of the opposite sex. Do you get turned on thinking about being made love to as a woman?" He didn't pause long enough for me to answer, for which I was deeply grateful. "Because you're a normal heterosexual male, I think this might be what's happened with you. You're aroused by women and by the thought of yourself as a woman, and we need to rewire that to fit a normal heterosexual male pattern."

"I am a woman," I said, but with less emphasis than I intended.

"Chris, I want you to pay attention to what you think about when you imagine yourself as a woman, and what role arousal plays in that, and come back next week prepared to talk about that."

I did the first part of that assignment. I couldn't help it. Once he suggested it, every time I thought about being a woman, I was questioning what I was really thinking about. But there was no way in hell I was going to talk to him about it.

CHAPTER TWENTY-THREE

CLAIRE

Chris was going downhill visibly as far as Claire could tell. After the second trip to Dr. Webber that summer, he stopped telling her what the appointments were about, but he was as upset as she'd ever seen him. He curled in on himself and stopped talking in full sentences when one-word answers would do. She dragged him out to movies, where he would slump down in the seat like a bag of sand. She couldn't tell if he was really watching the movie or brooding on what the doctor had said that week.

Since he wouldn't talk to her, she started doing research,

trying to figure out what the doctor could be saying to him. Obviously, Dr. Webber thought transsexualism could be cured, but how? What she found made her feel sick and miserably confused. She could understand why Chris looked like the undertaker of a medieval village struck by plague.

First there was a bunch of confusing scientific jargon that took her about four days to wade through. It proposed that there was a difference between men who got turned on wearing women's clothes, women who were born into male bodies, and men who got turned on by thinking about being women. That was enough to make anyone miserable, but then she found the Christian Medical Fellowship stuff.

Apparently some groups, mostly self-identified as Christians, believed that transsexualism and homosexuality arose when a child failed to bond properly with the parent of the same sex as themselves. This unbonded kid then became defensive toward all people of the same sex as themselves and in adolescence turned the distance between themselves and people of the same sex into desire for a loving bond. Which explained the group's perspective on gays, but she didn't quite see how that made any sense in Chris's situation.

If she had to make up an argument based on this crap, she would say that he failed to bond with men and had decided he wanted to be a woman, which sounded like what Dr. Webber was saying. It just felt wrong to her. First, she knew that Chris loved his dad and admired him, and he didn't seem to have trouble hanging out with the guys on the swim team. It just bothered him that everyone thought he was one of them.

More looking showed that reparative therapy for homosexuality had a pretty abysmal success rate. It might seem to work for some gays who were fundamentalist Christians or really hated themselves, but for everyone else, it did a lot more damage than "repair."

She was more interested in the Christian arguments, which went that God and Jesus's relationship with humanity was one of a groom to a bride, and that heterosexual marriages were a mirror of that and therefore represented God's plan for humanity.

That made her angry. They seemed to think that God's plan for humanity looked like 1950s America. How many of them had really studied what it was like in Biblical times when women were largely considered property? Men could take multiple wives, and marriages were essentially arranged by families, not by individuals.

And if you were going to interpret literally the idea that God's relationship to humanity was a groom's to a bride's, then wasn't everyone a woman in God's eyes? When had it become so important who was a man and who was a woman? It felt to Claire like a perversion of the beauty of God's love for humanity to make the relationship with God into something so constricting. But she also understood how, in her own life, discipline made creativity possible. Was it possible that these people could be right that God had a plan?

She shut down her computer and rubbed her eyes, her questions no more resolved after a week of research than they'd been when she started. She just wanted Chris to be okay, whatever that meant.

It was still light outside, because of the length of the summer days in Minnesota, and the air held the heat of the day. A half-mile from her house, a small stream wound its way between two thinly wooded banks. Claire headed there and walked along the stream until the trees started to thicken and she could sit, unnoticed, on a big rock at the edge of the water.

The highway wasn't far, and she heard the rush of cars behind the sound of the water, but she liked to sit here anyway and watch the leaves flutter and reveal palm-sized bits of sky. The trees didn't worry about the kinds of things she did. They just grew, and they seemed to know how to grow. They reminded her of the verse in Matthew: *Consider the lilies of the field, how they grow; they neither toil nor spin, yet I tell you, even Solomon in all his glory was not arrayed like one of these.*

At the end of the day, she believed in a God who took care of His people, not one who hurt and limited them without reason. It came down to a choice between two worlds. She could look for weeks for answers and still it would be a matter of faith and belief. What did she believe to be true about this world she lived in? Did she believe that God made some people homosexual and transsexual just so they would have to overcome that? Or did she believe in a God who so loved variety and diversity that He created all manner of things and loved them all as they were?

Put that way, the choice was clear. Her God had always been a loving God not a legalistic God. Jesus had said: *This is my commandment, that you love one another as I have loved you.* She was drawn to the image of Jesus as bridegroom by the same idea that captured her attention in the Song of Solomon where God was represented by the lover. It was that quality of love: deep, vast and unalterable. She knew God loved her that way and she tried her best to return it. Her relationship with Chris couldn't compare to that, but she tried to take care of him as best she knew how.

She realized that she might be the only person in Emily's life who could reflect to her the kind of love that God had for everyone. Maybe that's what she was here for. Unless it was really all about her learning to wear eye shadow.

Claire laughed and pushed herself up off the stone on the riverbank. Actually, in a way, it was both about Emily and eye shadow, she realized. Over the last six months she'd gone from being terrified and confused to knowing she would fight for Emily's right to be herself—and fighting for Emily was fighting for herself too.

Standing with the cooling air on her face, Claire saw the pattern coming together. Emily was just the visible edge but everyone had parts of themselves that they were afraid to show. The more she spoke up for Emily, the more Claire felt those parts in herself come forward: the vulnerable, soft, creative elements of her own being.

She thought of a half dozen spiritual quotes that expressed

that idea, but she didn't need to look up any of them. The connection between her and Emily and all the people in the world was for a moment shiningly clear in the early evening's golden sunlight.

CHAPTER TWENTY-FOUR

I thought we were going to a movie, but Claire told me to drive to Dr. Mendel's office. At first, I just stared at her because I couldn't figure out what movie theater or restaurant was anywhere near that office park. In addition, Claire was actually wearing a red T-shirt with her jeans, which made me wonder what was going on with her.

"Why?" I asked.

"Because you have an appointment," she said.

"No I don't."

"Come on, drive, we're going to be late. I made you an appointment with Dr. Mendel. Hit the gas."

As I turned the car in the direction of her office, my heart started lifting and the headache around my eyes relaxed. I didn't dare hope that I would get time with the doctor.

"How did you make me an appointment?" I asked Claire.

"It's called a telephone," she said. "You punch in numbers and someone answers, remember?"

At the office building she grabbed my hand and dragged me into the waiting room. Dr. Mendel smiled when she saw us sitting there, and I'm sure we were quite a sight with me slump-shouldered in my chair and Claire gripping my hand as if I was going to bolt. And I suppose if it had been Dr. Webber instead of Dr. Mendel, I would have. Instead I let Claire pull me into her room and push me toward the couch. Claire remained standing.

"Chris is all messed up," she told Dr. Mendel. "She won't tell me all of it, but I'm hoping she'll tell you. Dr. Webber's been saying some crap to her, and I think she's starting to buy it. Can you straighten her out? Err, so to speak."

"I'll try," Dr. Mendel said.

Her reading glasses hung over her chest, taking the place of the pearls that she wore when my parents came to the appointment. She had on a bluish lavender knit sweater with short sleeves and I loved the color. It made her bright blue eyes really stand out, but when she turned them to me, the lines around them were tight with concern.

"Great, I'll be waiting," Claire announced and skipped out of the room.

I stared at the closed door. "She just told me about this," I said.

"You don't look well," Dr. Mendel offered. She pulled her chair two feet closer to the couch and sat down close enough that I could have reached forward and touched her knee. "Have you been taking care of yourself?"

"No," I admitted. "Life has pretty much sucked after we left here. Mom grounded me for life, Dad doesn't talk much, I ran out of hormones so I'm a rage-monster again. And then I freaked out after this dinner thing. Well, Mom freaked out first, but I really lost it and started cutting up my boy clothes and beating the crap out of my door."

"You didn't hurt yourself?" she asked.

I shook my head. "I couldn't."

"That's good."

"And then they asked me to go back to Dr. Webber and said if I saw him for a month I could go get hormones."

"That's an interesting strategy," Dr. Mendel said neutrally. I got the impression that "interesting" was a euphemism for "screwed up."

"He's crazy," I told her. "He thinks he can cure me of my transsexualism. He thinks I get off on thinking about myself as a woman."

"What do you think?" Dr. Mendel asked. Something in her voice got me—the way she just asked and then got quiet to listen to me. She really wanted to know and whatever she believed, one way or the other, she wasn't going to push it on me.

I started crying. The tears felt hot on my cheeks, not like all the helpless tears I'd cried in the past few weeks, these were pure grief mixed with the hurt and rage and fear that I needed to get out of me. She handed me tissues and let me cry for what seemed like the whole hour.

"I don't think I'm crazy," I managed at last. "I don't think this is all in my head. I just know I'm a girl, that's all. Why is that so hard for everyone to understand?"

"Probably for many of the same reasons it was hard for you," she said, and I was able to smile because of how gently she reminded me that I'd had years to understand what it meant to be transsexual and my family only had a few weeks.

After a pause to let her words sink in, she continued. "I know there's a simple answer to this question, but I want you to look beyond it: why are you so hurt by what Dr. Webber says?"

"I feel insulted," I said, "but that's the simple answer. And I feel invalidated, like he doesn't really see me at all. And I'm afraid—sometimes, I'm afraid he might be right."

She nodded, so I went on.

"You know, I have some girl clothes that I've worn out in the world a few times, and before Mom went nuts sometimes I'd just get up in the middle of the night and put them on. I liked to surf the web and stuff when I was dressed like myself. But sometimes when I'd get dressed up in the girl clothes, I would get aroused, like Dr. Webber says. I get afraid that maybe I'm just deluding myself and maybe I am a guy who gets his kicks dressing up like a girl."

She nodded again. "You're worried that if you get an erection while wearing women's clothing that you're a fetishist or cross-dresser and not a real transsexual?"

"Yeah," I said, knowing I was blushing a deep beet color.

"You know there's no such thing as a test for a 'true transsexual' by which we could determine externally whether it's right for someone to transition or not. Only you can say if this is who you are and what you need," she said. "But I can tell you a few things that might help you answer it for yourself. There isn't a one-to-one connection between getting an erection sometimes and being aroused by the idea of wearing women's clothing. As I understand it, you're basically thrilled any time you get to participate in life as a girl."

"Of course," I said.

"And your body doesn't always know the difference between that excitement and arousal. Certainly not at your age with all the hormones you have coursing through your body as an adolescent. Have you noticed other times when you get an erection for seemingly no reason at all? Or when you're excited about something but not necessarily turned on sexually?"

"Yeah, I have."

"Do you find women's clothing sexually exciting?" she asked.

I thought about it. "Not really. I mean, not the clothes themselves. But sometimes when I'm in them I think about having a real woman's body and what that would feel like to be able to touch someone and be touched without feeling like the Frankenstein monster."

"Frankenstein?" she queried.

"Like I have extra parts clumsily bolted on," I said, so embarrassed by this whole conversation that I thought I'd probably melt through the floor before the session ended.

"That makes sense to me," she said. "As I said, you're the only one who can say what's going on in your mind, but I don't think it's unusual for a person who knows herself to be a woman to be aroused by the idea of being made love to as a woman. If you're aroused by the idea of being a man who presents as a woman, we should talk about that. For example, if some of the arousal comes from the idea of being discovered as a man, or perhaps being a man who is somehow forced into womanhood. Those are both also valid ways to be."

"No, I don't want to be a man at all, I never have."

She smiled. "No one else has the right to tell you who you are, no matter what degrees they have. Are you committed to going to the rest of your appointments with Dr. Webber?"

"I want the hormones, and that's the only way my parents are going to let me have them."

"Then let me give you one bit of advice, though I'm not in the habit of doing that: Don't get angry at the rain."

"What?"

"When it rains and you get wet, you just dry off again. You know it's not raining on you personally, so you don't get upset at it. You know the rain falls on everyone the same way. You just take whatever steps you need to dry off and take care of yourself. Dr. Webber is like that. He's just raining and it's falling on you, but it's not personal. He would treat any teen who came to him and said 'I'm transsexual' that way; he's not addressing who you are, Emily, as an individual."

I'd have hugged her, but she was a therapist and I didn't know if that was cool, so when we stood up I just shook her hand for a long time. Before I opened the door, I paused. "My mom and dad don't know I'm here, do they?"

"I doubt it, Claire set up the appointment and paid for it."

"She paid for it? Wow. Can I do that too?"

"Of course you can. Just call a few days in advance and we'll set it up."

I slipped out to the waiting room and half-lifted Claire out of her chair into a huge hug.

"Hey it worked," she exclaimed. "I got you back."

I kissed her. "You're a great protector," I said.

"Claire the Mighty," she grinned.

***

I couldn't say I was looking forward to the next trip to Dr. Webber, but at least I wasn't dreading it quite so much. I even played with him a little bit. At one point I volunteered, "I'll tell you some of the fantasies I have about being a woman."

"Go on," he said.

I was trying hard not to smile. "In one, I go out to dinner with my girlfriend, Claire, and the waiter says 'What would you ladies like to order?' Oh, and then there's the one where I'm shopping, and I go to use the women's restroom and there's another woman in there and she looks at me and says 'Nice shoes.'"

Mostly I put up with him trying to guy-bond with me, and talked about my childhood memories of my dad. Dr. Mendel's advice made a big difference in the visits too. No matter how stupid they got, I'd come home and take a shower and imagine washing off any crap he said, and then I'd towel off and imagine I was drying off the rain.

"It's not personal," I'd look at myself in the mirror and say until it sank in. And then I'd go down to dinner.

Most of August was one of the strangest times of my life. Now that I was out to my parents, I didn't try so hard to act like a guy. Slowly, I started being myself as best I could and a weight lifted off my shoulders and skull. Around the house, though, my self-expression met with mixed results

"There is no way Sabretooth could beat Starfire in one-on-

one," I told Mikey one evening as we sat at dinner, punctuating my points with finger jabs. "If Cyclops can blast him away, so can Starfire." I illustrated the rising and falling arc of Sabretooth's defeated body.

"Well what about Nightcrawler versus Starfire," Mikey shot back. "He can teleport."

I was grinning at him, but I felt the hair on the back of my next standing up and looked over to see Mom glaring at me.

"Stop waving your hands around," she snapped.

I crossed my arms and turned back to Mikey. "I think that would be a cool fight to watch," I told him.

A moment later when Mom went to the garage to get Dad for dinner, Mikey whispered, "I bet no one yells at Starfire like that."

I grinned and ruffled his hair. "I bet you're right."

Dad never said anything, but twice while he was watching TV with Mikey and me, he simply got up and left the room. When he didn't come back, I reviewed the last few minutes in my mind and realized he left right after I crossed my legs above the knee and folded my hands together in my lap.

***

One afternoon in the middle of the month, when I went into the garage to see what Dad was doing, he put down his wrench and sat back on his heels. "I made you an appointment," he said brusquely. "You need to send a letter."

It took me a minute to figure out what he was talking about. "The endocrinologist?" I asked, incredulous.

"Yes, he's in the Cities. I'm going with you. If he says this isn't safe, I want you to promise me you're not going to make a fuss. You're going to do what the doctor says."

"Of course." I skipped across the room and put my arms

around his shoulders, giving him a kiss on the cheek. "Thanks, Dad."

"And you need to talk to that doctor, the one you like, she has to send him some kind of letter about you."

"No problem, I'll do it," I told him.

He grumbled something I couldn't hear and got back under the car. Knowing I had that appointment to look forward to made the last couple weeks with Dr. Webber bearable. Mom came back in with me one time to complain that I was acting effeminate around the house.

"I'm not acting," I said, but it fell on deaf ears. Dr. Webber suggested that my Dad should take me to more sporting events and that the family should go to church together. We did end up going to church, but I brought Claire and she actually enjoyed it, so that made it easy to sit through.

Finally the big day rolled around. Dad put on a suit coat to take me in to see the doctor. He only had two of them, and I was glad that I got the gray one for church and not his black formal dinner and funerals jacket. I wore my usual jeans, but dug out a nice T-shirt. I wondered if I should wear something more feminine, but I was already on eggshells with Mom. I had given Dad the names of two doctors that had been recommended to me by Dr. Mendel, and he went with one of those, so I was sure this doctor had a good sense about transsexualism and how to treat it.

On the drive in, I couldn't keep my legs still. When I tried to stop them, my right hand danced up and down my thigh, picking at the seam of my jeans. Finally I managed to settle on wiggling my toes in my shoes on one foot and then the other, back and forth. I could tell Dad was tense too, because he didn't bother to try to make small talk. We listened to the radio most of the way, or at least tried to.

Funny thing: the appointment was just like the physical exams I'd gotten every year since I could remember. The nurse checked my blood pressure, weight, temperature, all that stuff, and then put me in a little room to wait for the doctor. Dad came in with me because he had questions.

The doctor walked in reading my file. He was an Indian man with short, very black hair, thick black eyebrows and an even thicker black mustache. His white coat and the bright blue and white striped dress shirt underneath it gave his brown skin a slightly gray hue. He pushed his rectangular wire frame glasses up on his nose with one hand and closed the file, then introduced himself to Dad and me.

"Looks like you're in good health," he said very matter-of-factly and without any hint of an accent. "I received the letter from Dr. Mendel about your transsexualism. You want to go on HRT?"

"Yes, totally."

He smiled then, which made him look a lot younger than my dad all of a sudden. I wondered if the mustache was an attempt to look older. He had a handsome, wide mouth and perfect teeth.

"Well, Chris, I'd like to put you on a dose of Spironolactone, fifty milligrams twice a day. That will reduce the amount of testosterone in your blood to normal female levels. I'm also going to put you on Premarin starting at two and a half milligrams a day and then doubling that. Now some people think more is better when it comes to estrogen, but that is just not the case. Taking more won't make the process any faster. You need to stick to this regimen. Okay?"

"Yes," I said. "No problem."

Dad shifted in his chair. "You're just going to give him the hormones? Just like that? Are they dangerous? What do they do?"

The doctor leaned back against the white table that ran along one wall and folded his arms loosely into what seemed to be his lecture pose. "There are risks, as there are with any medication. Chris is in excellent health, and we'll want him back here every few months to make sure his liver and kidneys are processing the hormones well."

"It's reversible, right?" Dad asked.

"More or less, yes," the doctor said. "Chris will start to notice his skin softening, his body hair will become less heavy. Over a period of a few months to a year the fat on his body will start to redistribute itself. His face will look softer, and he will start to develop breasts."

"Good Lord," Dad said. A muscle clenched in the side of his jaw and he shook his head, but didn't say more.

"Up to that point, he can stop taking the hormones and the changes will reverse themselves. Once he's developed breasts… well, you need surgery to reverse that."

Dad's normally tan face was turning blotchy, parts becoming pink and other parts a faint yellowish green.

"Dad, please …"

He sat back against the wall and didn't say anything. And that was it. The doctor wrote out the prescriptions and told us to come back in a few months. I made Dad stop at the first Walgreens we saw and fill the prescriptions. Then I took one of each of the pills with a candy bar and bottle of water to wash them down.

"Do you want to go to a movie?" Dad asked when I got back in the car.

"That'd be cool."

I thought he'd say something more about the doctor's visit, but he didn't. He just took us down the street to a theater and bought two tickets to the latest James Bond flick. I wondered if this was another last-ditch attempt to indoctrinate me back into manhood, but I didn't really care.

Sitting in the theater reminded me of being out with Claire and Natalie, and I wondered how Natalie was doing. She'd gone in for her surgery a few weeks back and I'd seen a few short posts from her on GenderPeace, but she'd been pretty out of it.

When we got out of the movie, I figured it wouldn't hurt to ask. "Dad, while we're down here, can we go see Natalie? She had to have some surgery this summer, and I'd like to see how she's doing."

"She live around here?" he asked. "We can't stay long. I promised your mom we'd be home for dinner."

"She's just a couple miles away."

As I rang her doorbell, I wondered if it was a bad idea to stop by unannounced, but it was one of the downfalls of not having a cell phone. Natalie's mom answered the door with a big smile and immediately my pounding heart slowed down. I'd been afraid that if her dad answered, he wouldn't be cool about the visit at all, though I didn't know that for sure.

Natalie's mom had her hair tied back again and wore the same kind of outfit she had on for the slumber party: loose black pants and a law school sweatshirt. She stepped to the side of the doorway and waved us in.

"What a surprise!" she said and held her hand out to my father. "It's good to see you again, please come in."

"Thank you," Dad replied and gave her hand a quick shake. His gaze traveled around the foyer. Their house was a lot nicer than ours—not much bigger, but I knew he was looking at the building materials and how nice they were. The foyer was paved with a fine gray stone and the windows on either side of the door had stained glass patterns in them.

"Jerry, would you like to join me in the kitchen for a coffee while the kids talk?" she asked. "I just made a pot."

"Thank you," he said again.

To me she said, "Natalie's upstairs in her room, first one on the left, go on up. I know she'd love to see you."

I bounded up the stairs. At the top I paused, outside the left-hand door, and knocked lightly.

"Who is it?" Natalie asked weakly.

"Emily," I announced through the door.

"Hey!" Her voice picked up volume. "Get in here!"

I pushed open the door. Her room was a rich palette of cream colors and light browns with a bed dominating the far wall where Natalie sat propped amid teddy bears. Two flower arrangements flanked the bed, and I felt stupid that Claire and I hadn't thought to come out together and bring one. We should have visited sooner, and now Claire was going to be mad that she didn't get to come on this trip. Natalie's hair frizzed out from her head in a dark halo, and she looked very monochrome with no makeup on, but she was smiling.

"Sit down," she said, gesturing to the chair next to the bed. "Are you just dropping by?"

"Dad brought me in to get hormones, can you believe it?"

She laughed. "That's great."

"So how is it?" I asked. "What's it like? How do you feel?"

"It hurts," she said, still grinning. "It hurts a hell of a lot. But I wouldn't trade it for the world."

"Tell me everything."

"Well, first I had to go off hormones for two weeks, which sucked as you can imagine. Then Mom and Robin and I flew to Arizona—"

"Robin?"

"My sister. She said she'd make it more like a holiday for Mom so she didn't freak out while I was in surgery. Then I got prepped and shaved and they ran all these tests, and then they put me under. And when I woke up I felt…I don't really know how to describe it. I mean, I was high on all the drugs, so I was feeling pretty happy anyway, but separate from that I felt whole.

"That first day out wasn't so bad, but then the heavy drugs wore off and it hurt like a bitch. Plus the strong painkillers made me sick, and let me tell you that puking after that surgery is unbelievably awful. But after a couple days I could get up and walk a few steps, and after that I started feeling better pretty quickly. I'm still sore, and I'm supposed to take it easy for a few more days, but I walk around some every day now. And, wow, it's so different. I mean, for the last two years I've been living as a girl, but with this terrible freakish part that I always had to hide and pay attention to, you know. It's just weird. And now, I'm just me. And in some way I always was, except it all fits together now."

"Cool," I said, feeling envious, but also afraid. I wasn't a big fan of surgery in general.

"How are you?" she asked, and I updated her about all the craziness in my life since I'd told my parents, until Natalie's mom poked her head through the door and said it was time for me to go.

I gave Natalie a gentle hug.

"I'm excited for you," she said.

"Same here," I said and laughed. She made me promise to come visit again when she was up and around more. With school starting in a week, it would be a lot easier to get around without Mom watching my every move. I felt sure that a visit to my T-girl friend wasn't on the list of Dr. Webber-approved activities for me.

In the car on the way back to Liberty, Dad didn't say much, but what he said gave me an idea about what he and Natalie's mom had been talking about in the kitchen.

"You didn't tell me Natalie used to be a boy," he said.

"No," I said. "She's just a regular girl now. That's how she wants people to see her. She doesn't go around with a big 'T' on her chest."

"T?" he asked.

"For transsexual."

"I wouldn't have known," he said.

I didn't know what to say to that, so I didn't say anything. I wasn't sure if he was going down Mom's well-worn track about how I'd make an ugly woman, or if he was trying to say something else. When we got home I made sure I thanked him a couple times for taking me to the doctor.

CHAPTER TWENTY-FIVE

School starting brought a welcome relief to the whole family. Despite the high temperatures of the summer, the house had been emotionally cold as a tomb since June. I dove into my classes with fervor, and started going over to Claire's most nights after school, except for the dreaded Wednesdays when I still had to see crazy Dr. Webber. He'd been taking lots of notes during my visits of late, and I started to feel paranoid. I had to figure out a way to stop seeing him, but for most of September I was content just to have my regular life back, except without as much lying and pretending as I'd had to do a year ago.

I fantasized about telling my swim coach the real reason I was quitting the team. I imagined walking into his office and saying, "Actually, here's the truth. I'm a transsexual woman and I'm going to start growing breasts this year, so I can't swim with the guys any more." Unfortunately, the second part of that imagined scenario involved him outing me to the whole school, so I never went with that plan. Instead I pointed out that I wasn't in the top half of the team and said that I needed to focus on schoolwork and earning money for college. He argued against it, but I was tenacious.

I didn't know if I could refuse to go to Dr. Webber without Mom trying to cut off my supply of hormones, but I had to try. After Claire and I brainstormed over the weekend, I cornered Mom in her tiny office after dinner on Sunday.

I tried to sound as plaintive as possible, and not demanding. "Mom, I really don't want to go to Dr. Webber anymore, he gives me the creeps."

"That was the deal," she said. "You get to see your doctor, but you have to see mine too."

I sat on the edge of her desk. "When we have appointments and you're not there, he spends the whole time asking about my sexual fantasies," I said. "It's gross."

Now she turned in her chair to look at me. "Are you lying to me, Christopher?"

"I'm not," I said. "I mean, you know I can't stand him, but if that was it, I could keep going I suppose. He makes me feel disgusting. He wants to talk about masturbation and stuff. It's nasty. And then he takes lots and lots of notes. I'm afraid of what he's going to do with them. Can we just find another doctor? You can pick one who wants to change me, just not a…you know, a gross one."

She sighed. "I don't know why you persist in this delusion about womanhood," she said. "What do you think it's going to solve? Do you think your life would be easier as a woman?"

I sagged against the desk, holding myself up with my arms. After months of this, even the first few lines of my mother's argument made me feel as if I'd gone three days without sleeping. "It's not going to make my life easier," I said. "Are you kidding?"

"Then why?" she asked.

"Because I *am* a woman," I said simply. "That's all. What would you do if you'd grown up as a boy?"

"I'd be a boy," she said. "I wouldn't be myself. That's the point, Chris, people don't go from one to the other. You're not a woman. You don't act like a woman, you don't think like a woman. I'm afraid you're just going to turn out to be a freak, and you'll never get what you're really looking for."

Normally, I would have fought with her and insisted that I am a woman and therefore I think like one and so on. But I didn't. Maybe it was the mellow weekend I'd had, or the hormones I was taking, or being able to be honest to more people than I ever had before, but I didn't feel angry at her like I usually did. I could start to understand that she honestly wanted me to be happy and she just didn't see how all this could work.

"I'm afraid of that too," I admitted. "I'm afraid I'll get through all this and I won't look or sound like a woman."

"Then why do it?" she asked plaintively.

"Because being treated like a guy all the time, having to pretend I am a guy, I'm lying to everyone. It destroys me. I would rather fail at being myself than succeed at being someone I'm not."

She shook her head. "I don't understand it, and I'm still going to look for another way out for you."

"But not Dr. Webber?"

"No," she said. "Not him. But you're still going to church at least twice a month."

I enjoyed church with Claire explaining it all to me, but I knew I had to pretend it was a chore. "Ugh, Mom," I said and sighed heavily. "Fine. If I have to."

I thought the talk went well, and I was elated to have the weight of Dr. Webber off me, but Mom's comment about me not thinking like a woman haunted me. Was it possible that even though I felt female inside, my growing up as boy had changed me forever? Would I never fit in anywhere except for the transgender community? Although I found support there, I couldn't imagine living my whole life inside those boundaries.

I asked Claire about it, and she quickly pried out of me the details of the entire conversation with my mother. Then she almost fell out of her chair laughing. We were sitting alone at the end of a long table in the cafeteria talking in whispers. We'd arranged our lunch periods together this year. I think that our highly visible joy at being together was the only factor that kept the other kids at school from deciding I was gay.

"Why are you laughing?" I demanded.

"Let me get this straight," she said. "In the middle of a conversation in which you got out of seeing Dr. Webber by insinuating that he has a sexual interest in you, your mother suggests you don't think like a woman. I don't know what girl manual your mom got, but that's in the first five pages of mine. That's totally a girl trick. No self-respecting straight teen guy would suggest some man was leering at him to get his way."

I said in my best Valley Girl impression, "So, I'm, like, totally a girl."

"You're certainly more of a girl than I am," she said. "You actually like makeup." She rolled her eyes. "You're like an eleven-year-old worried that you're never going to get your period. Chill out."

I made myself sigh and look down at my plate and frown.

"What?" she asked with a hint of real concern.

"You're right, I am afraid I'm never going to get my period," I said.

***

The strangest thing happened a few days after Christmas. Mom was going through another phase of not really talking to me, and Claire had gotten her acceptance letter to that university in Iowa with the really good writing program. It was pretty clear we weren't going to be together after next summer, so I was just bummed. She said she'd always be my best friend, but I couldn't imagine what I was going to do without her. I didn't have the money to go to a really good school and if I did have the money, I'd spend it on surgery anyway, so I figured I'd go to a community college for a two-year degree and then transfer to the University of Minnesota for the last two years. By then I planned to be living as a woman full time.

But that remained a long way off and so my Christmas was bleak. Claire went to visit her dad, and I was stuck in the house with Mom glaring at me every time I did something girlish and with Dad wrapped up in his cars.

Two days after Christmas while I was slumped on the couch trying to be interested in the television, Dad opened the door to the garage and said, "Come here."

I got up and followed him into his workshop that was, as usual, littered with tools and car parts. He picked a small, badly gift-wrapped box off his worktable and tossed it at me.

"What's this?" I asked.

"Late Christmas present," he said. "Open it."

I did. It was a small box with a set of car keys. "Dad, I already have a car."

Standing next to me, he turned me toward the 1977 Ford Thunderbird he'd been working on. It was still a bit of a monstrosity, but, as he often boasted, for something he'd picked up for twenty-five hundred bucks, who could complain. It had good lines and with the right paint job it would look slick.

"Now you have two," he said.

"What am I going to do with two cars?"

"Sell one of 'em. What do you think you can get for the Chevy?"

I felt my jaw loosening, wanting to drop open. "Sixteen," I said with effort. "Maybe seventeen grand."

"Good," he said. "There you go."

"For school?" I asked, still not quite believing my ears.

"For whatever you want. I don't need to know what you use it for."

Was he suggesting I use it to pay for surgery?

"Dad—?" I started.

He turned to face me fully. "Look Chris, I don't understand this stuff you're into. It makes no sense to me. All I know is that you've been angry and sad damn near your whole life, and now you're happy. I want you to stay that way. You do whatever you need. And if I hurt you when you were little…well, I'm sorry."

I started crying. I couldn't talk.

He threw an arm over my shoulders and tightened it once. "Jesus Christ," he said roughly.

After a minute he dropped his arm and walked across the workshop to his latest project. "What do you think I can get for this shit?" he yelled back to me. "It's shot to hell."

I wiped my face and walked over to where he was standing. "It's worth something," I said. "I'll look it up."

He didn't bring the topic up again, but I spent more time over that holiday working on the cars with him and a couple times I could have sworn he'd stopped calling me "son" and started calling me "hon."

***

I kept my head down through most of the winter, and toward the end of it, Mom seemed to have relaxed. She might have thought I was growing out of my "transsexual phase" as she once put it, because I had resolved not to bring it up until I could move out of the house.

One evening in late January Claire and I were having dinner in front of her TV. Claire's mom was now seriously dating the man she'd started seeing the previous summer and as a result was out late a couple nights a week. Whenever Claire saw such a night coming, she made sure I came over and let me wear whatever I wanted. I was in the Banana Republic pants Natalie had picked out and a knit sweater Claire got me for Christmas.

"Hey," she said on a commercial and muted the TV. "Know what today is?"

"Did I miss an anniversary?"

"Only of the night you came out to me."

"Wow."

"Thanks," she said. "For trusting me and all that."

I just pulled her close. One year since I'd come out to her and my family, and I'd met all sorts of friends in the Cities. I had a therapist and a plan. Not too shabby.

"Are you getting weepy?" Claire asked from my shoulder. "Don't cry on me. You are such a girl."

"Me? You're the one wearing eye shadow to watch TV."

"You put it on me."

We gaped at each other in mock horror and then fell together laughing.

"Seeing you have to fight for all this," she said. "It makes me appreciate more what I have."

I kissed the top of her head. "Glad I could help."

"Yeah, my mom says you're a good influence. She loves you," she said, laughing. Then she paused and I could feel her warm breath fluttering over my collarbone. "I love you," she said.

I tightened my hold on her. Small as she was, she'd been the most solid part of my life during the last year. I didn't have the words to tell her what it meant to me that through all of this we still got to be people sitting together and just laughing or crying or kissing each other.

EPILOGUE

THREE YEARS LATER

    Claire and I went off to our separate colleges, not without envy on my part and a lot of loneliness for both of us. We tried to keep dating, but by that first Christmas, it was pretty obviously not going to work. So I put my nose down into my books and pulled a brilliant GPA while saving up as much money as I could. Weekends I got to be myself in the city, and on longer breaks I made some friends I could stay with there, including Elizabeth from the support group. She let me stay at the guest room in her house over spring break and for a few weeks in the summer as I got used to living as a girl for longer periods of time.

I now have a two-year degree and am in the middle of my first year at the University of Minnesota. I enrolled here as Emily Christine Hesse and only a couple of people in admissions and the health office know I didn't grow up as a girl. I had the facial surgery last summer and pretty much look like I did except that my nose is a lot cuter and I don't have the caveman brow ridge; I now look like I did before I hit puberty and testosterone messed everything up. Claire came with me for the surgery and read me some of her writing while I recovered. She says I look like Jennifer Garner, which is ridiculous. But I do look good.

I have some of the money in the bank for my last surgery and I'm hoping to have it next summer when I have plenty of time to recover so I don't mess up my schoolwork. I'll also use that time to edit this account that I've written of that crazy year when I came out and set myself to growing into the woman I am. Claire's helped out by telling me her parts of the story, and I've tried to reflect the whole tale as completely and fairly as possible.

Oh, and speaking of fairness, Mom turned out to be okay with her new daughter. She took an entire two years to come around. I think she felt like Chris died, and didn't know how to grieve that. But she thinks I do look pretty great as a girl.

It's weird to still be in an in-between place, with one more surgery to go. I'm eager and a little scared.

The waiting and all the trouble has been more than made up for by the fact that the pencil outline of my life has been filled in and I get to walk around campus fully visible and luminous as myself.

Claire actually says it all better than I do, but you'll have to read her book for that whole story. She says that when she's around me now she can see that I'm in a state of wonder about life itself; I don't take any day for granted. I don't know if I would have done this life any differently if I had a choice. I don't know anyone who appreciates a hot bath like I do, or the feel of my hair on the back of my neck when I turn, or the way my heart lifts into the back of my eyes when anyone says "Excuse me, miss."

Claire says she used to think ordinary life was boring before I came out to her, but now she realizes that every ordinary moment has extraordinary worlds contained within it. But then she's the mystic. I'll take my ordinary moments and enjoy every one of them.